Last Summer on State Street

Last Summer on State Street

A Novel

Toya Wolfe

wm

WILLIAM MORROW
An Imprint of HarperCollins*Publishers*

HarperCollins books may be purchased for educational, business, or sales promotional use. For information, please email the Special Markets Department at SPsales@harpercollins.com.

FIRST EDITION

Designed by Kyle O'Brien

Library of Congress Cataloging-in-Publication Data

Names: Wolfe, Toya, author.
Title: Last summer on State Street : a novel / Toya Wolfe.
Description: First edition. | New York : William Morrow an imprint of HarperCollins, [2022]
Identifiers: LCCN 2021038047 | ISBN 9780063209749 (hardback) | ISBN 9780063209756 (ebook)
Subjects: LCGFT: Bildungsromans.
Classification: LCC PS3623.O366 L37 2022 | DDC 813/.6—dc23
LC record available at https://lccn.loc.gov/2021038047

ISBN 978-0-06-320974-9

22 23 24 25 26 LSC 10 9 8 7 6 5 4 3 2 1

For Diane and Diane

Two things everybody's got tuh do fuh theyselves. They got tuh go tuh God, and they got tuh find out about livin' fuh theyselves.

—Zora Neale Hurston,
Their Eyes Were Watching God

Last Summer on State Street

Prologue

I'd known Precious forever, Stacia a year, and Tonya for just a minute. We were *so* different, but everybody loved them some double Dutch. Sometimes we made a tight-knit crew; other days we couldn't get along for nothing.

Our friendships started with "What's your name?" The answer carried with it looks that I can still see clearly: Stacia's begged me not to talk to her, and Tonya's asked, "Is she talking to me?!" We got past those facial expressions and gave our names. Names that sound like heartbeats: *Fe Fe, Precious, Stacia, Tonya.*

It's kind of a miracle that we formed those bonds, because our mothers couldn't stand each other. To this day, I wonder how me and Precious were cool for so long. And Stacia? Everybody had something negative to say about the Buchanan family. I knew there'd be backlash for bringing Tonya around, but I couldn't know, at twelve, how bad things would get.

That summer, one by one, they dropped out of sight as if we were in a game of All in Together.

When you play All, you get two people to turn the rope, and then a ton of kids, it could be eight of us, we'd all jump in. The people turning sing, *All, All, All, All,* and repeat the word until there's no more room in the rope. Precious and I began that song before we could even walk.

Stacia jumped in when we started sixth grade, and Tonya appeared months later, in the middle of June. The song went on, and we jumped, screaming the lyrics, attempting to overpower the sounds of construction vehicles as they dismantled our South Side neighborhood in the Robert Taylor Homes.

> *All in together, any kind of weather*
> *I see teachers*
> *Looking out the window*
> *Ding, dong, the fire bell*
> *January, February,*
> *March, April, May, June, July . . .*

When we played the game, people left the rope one at a time, reliably, when they heard their birthday month. But in real life, their departures were sudden. Tonya got pulled out of the rope, and not long after her disappearance, Stacia vanished too. Precious stuck around until pretty late in the summer, like her birthday was in August, and then she just slid out and rode away in her family's Camry.

They left me standing there with the rope.

After all these years, I can still hear their voices screaming, "First!" "Second!" and "Zero no higher!" and arguing over who said "Zero no higher" first. The memories won't go away; they're proof that once upon a time, I lived in a brick skyscraper on State Street, in a place where stairwells filled with echoes of stamped-ing gym shoes and harmonizing winos. Those memories won't let me believe that I dreamt up Precious, Stacia, and Tonya, but All in Together is over.

ONE

The Square

By the summer of 1999, me, Precious, and Stacia—all twelve years old—ran around in this tight formation, snapping through the block in neon colors like a school of tropical fish. Sometimes you'd catch us flowing through the masses of guys in white tees on a quick trip to buy candy from Ms. Rose, or at Food & Liquor. There were dudes draped around the building's opening, standing guard in the parking lot, the tunnel inside the building leading to the stairway, everywhere, really. All the spaces around the building belonged to them, but we had our own spot, and for the longest time, no one bothered us there.

If you drove up the 90/94, a highway built to separate Blacks and whites without Jim Crow language, the Robert Taylor Homes loomed off to the side of your car. The buildings stared you down, their windows like eyes, watching. Off the highway, on State Street, the number 29 bus would take you on a ghetto tour, passing all those projects. You would see building after building and people just standing around.

Half the structures were off-white, the other ones, rust colored, and they'd alternate: red buildings, then a few white, then red, then white, then red, and it would go on like that for two miles.

From the exterior, these brick towers shot up sixteen stories in the air with neat rows of windows on one side and on the other, iron gates running the length of each floor, creating an opportunity for the residents to see out into the world and for people outside to catch a glimpse of project life.

The elevator moved up and down the middle of each building in an enclosed column of brick, and that's where my friends and I gathered, on the third floor, in that covered square of space. Though it housed the elevators, it was also spacious enough for people to carry their trash and large items they needed to dispose of. We were grateful for its large, smooth, cement floor, wide enough for our crew to run around and, most importantly, to jump rope.

I watched the traffic flow in and out and around the square. That summer, all these new faces popped up; they had moved from closed-up high-rises. On both sides of us, up and down State Street, there were blocks that looked like someone had dropped a bomb, leaving the destruction of brick towers. The wires clawed out from the sides of the high-rises that were ripped open, exposing colorful walls of vacated apartments. It seemed random, the Chicago Housing Authority's choice of which buildings to destroy first; some blocks—like mine—were completely intact, others a mess. I'd seen these horror scenes from the State Street bus on trips downtown and knew that the construction vehicles would appear on our block someday, but *someday* could be translated into *never* when you're a kid.

Once a building had been attacked, falling apart in this way, the residents were already settled into other project buildings or out in other parts of the city. Some people were relocated into my building, 4950. I kept an eye on these strangers but always watched for this one girl. She walked up and down the stairs all day. I couldn't tell her grade, mostly because she had a body all curved and rounded out like a grown woman. I bet, that summer, she had developed fast, because she seemed to be bursting out of what was probably a free D.A.R.E. T-shirt she'd gotten at school. Some girls loved to show off their bodies, but she didn't have that kind of energy. Instead, she acted more like a small, timid child.

We didn't look like her; Stacia and I were bony, with no curves at our hips and bumps for breasts. Precious hadn't shed her baby fat and still looked like a little kid. Even Tonya's skin color was different. Her complexion was a few shades darker than Precious's but still considered light, while Stacia and I were much darker. The four of us represented a gorgeous spectrum of tones.

She'd walk down the stairs, then I'd see her coming up again a few minutes later. The building served breakfast in the summertime on the first floor, so tons of people went by in the mornings going to Chokes—that's what everybody called the food, though it actually wasn't that bad. Sometimes, only ten minutes passed between her coming and going. Other days, I wouldn't see her again until night. She rarely looked over at the square. It was like she couldn't even see us. Then one day, as she passed our floor, she slowed down a little and looked over at us, as if she was going to say something, then she kept marching up the stairs.

I let go of both ends of the rope and ran after her. I caught up with her on the stairway landing between the third and fourth floors, and shouted, "What's your name?"

She turned around, raised her hands up as high as her ears, and backed up against the cinder block wall. Her eyes popped as

wide as they could go. I took a step back and said, "My name Fe
Fe." Then I asked her again, this time slower, and not so loud. She
let her shoulders ease a little, and her eyes went back to normal.

"Tonya."

I looked down the stairs and saw Precious's and Stacia's faces.
Stacia, a puddle of attitude, had her neck all stuck out and a hand
on one of her hips. Precious just seemed confused about why I'd
dashed up the stairs after a girl we didn't know.

All the signs were there, that this was a terrible idea, but I ignored them, and asked Tonya, "You want to play rope with me and
my friends?" Her eyes widened again, but this time, out of shock.

Stacia had heard enough and stomped away from the stairs,
audibly sharing her disgust at what I'd just asked Tonya. Precious
remained, understanding what I was about to do.

The year before, I'd invited Stacia to join our little duo. In the
building, it had been Precious and me for most of our lives. Our
other friends were kids we saw in specific places, like at school
or the girls that Precious saw on the weekends at church. For
as long as I'd known her, Precious had a sweet spirit, and made
friends easily, so even though Stacia was a Buchanan, and we had
all heard that they were bullies, Precious didn't mind playing with
Stacia.

Stacia was different: very territorial of her people and things.

Tonya moved toward me, and when she was inches away, I
could smell her, a combination of soured milk and armpit funk.
She had a shiny jelly stain on her T-shirt.

We walked back into the square, where Stacia and Precious
huddled together, whispering. I raised my voice, smothering them
out. "This Stacia. That's Precious. This Tonya." The tension made
the square seem cramped, and I tried my best to get everybody's
mood back up.

"Stacia, can you pick the next song?" I knew it would be something vulgar.

"Tonya, you can get on the end, it's Precious's turn." And for a second, they'd forgotten that I'd pulled in a new girl without asking if it was cool.

It was kind of a betrayal to open up a friendship, something so private and special, and walk a stranger in like that; Stacia's facial expression and body language confirmed this very notion. I didn't know that things wouldn't ever smooth over, that it would be so hard to fold in Tonya. In fact, the day our crew grew to four, that's when everything terrible started. It was like Tonya was the catalyst for the summer's events. I'd blame Stacia, but sometimes I wonder if Tonya was the real omen. I feel bad for thinking this way, but I can't help it.

With four people, we could play Beat, competing to see who jumped the longest, and wouldn't have to turn the rope. Days later, when Stacia got in my face about inviting "that dirty girl" to play with us, this was the reason that I gave, but truthfully, it had little to do with jumping rope. Tonya reminded me of Stacia when I met her, a kid with no friends. My heart went out to her, this lonely-looking girl; I wanted to help her. If I told that to Stacia, I knew she wouldn't care. That summer, Stacia watched Tonya go up and down the stairs too. Sometimes, Stacia would roll her eyes at her or just make a face as if she'd tasted something awful. This may be why, before today, Tonya stopped looking at us at all and passed by our double Dutch game without a glance.

Maybe because of the disruption of meeting Tonya, or because there was a stranger among us, Precious wasn't feeling so confident in her ability to jump into the rope the regular way. Usually, she'd run in while the ropes were going, but that day she said, "I want to stand in." So while the ropes lay limp on the ground, she stood in the middle of them, then we slowly rocked them back and forth, saying, "Ready, set, aaand . . . go!"

Stacia couldn't "run in" either. She could jump pretty well, but the challenge was getting her in the ropes. For a while, she had to stand next to one of the turners and dig potatoes, her hands scooping the air as she rocked toward and away from the ropes but not actually jumping in. The more time she spent digging, the angrier she got. When she finally jumped in, there was almost always a bad landing, and somebody got snapped on. That day, I knew it would be Tonya.

"She can't turn!" Stacia said, the ropes looped around her shoulders and torso as if she were a lassoed criminal. "You can get that over," I said. She freed herself, then tried it again. The real trouble started when Tonya got off the end and jumped into the rope without any problems. She knew how to crisscross *and* all-around. She made it through the song about George Washington, then the alphabet. When we got to numbers, Stacia couldn't take it anymore. The rope stopped, and Tonya got whacked across her arm. Her hand flew up to the spot, and she cringed. Maybe if Stacia's face looked concerned, even a little, I would've believed that it was an accident, but she smiled and sang, "Your turn, Fee!"

"No it ain't. She get that over," I said.

"Why?"

"Because *you* messed up her turn."

My friendship with Stacia was always exhausting, but the day that Tonya joined us, I worked overtime trying to keep the peace.

When Precious stepped in to help, saying, "Let's play Down Down Baby!" that defused the tension, and I was grateful that Precious was there. We rushed together and danced and sang. After each cheer, somebody would yell out, "Rockin' Robin," or

"Slide," and we got in position and sang and danced. Tonya already knew the words.

So, for a few hours, we had fun, without any more drama. Jumping rope and playing these hand games were our only real distraction from the ongoing demolition of the neighborhood, and as much as we could bury our heads in this joy, we did.

THE FOUR OF US SANG these same songs and played these same games even though we grew up in three different buildings. While our high-rises looked the same, how they were run, the people that lived in them, even the varying levels of structural damage— some had endured fires or were marked by different graffiti— distinguished them.

Stacia's family had to relocate from 4848 at the beginning of that school year because the buildings on her block were coming down, and Tonya moved into our building from 4946—which was one of the other two buildings on my block—because her old building was being demolished that summer.

All three of our buildings could've been three different countries, where people spoke their own slang, with unique customs, led by whichever gang ruled them. But since our families had all migrated from small towns in Mississippi, bringing the same superstitions, games, and cheers with them on those Illinois Central trains, we had these common things in our DNA; that's what glued us together for a time.

TWO

In War

After Precious calmed things down, we went back to jumping rope and played round after round, sometimes singing songs, other times jumping and listening to the sounds of the block. Woody and Earl were winos, but they could really sing. We loved the way their voices sounded in the stairway, a layered echo. They sang songs that we recognized as the "dusties" that made the soundtrack of our hairdos and cleaning days. My mama couldn't get anything done without listening to V103, her favorite radio station. This day, Woody and Earl harmonized a tune from the Spinners called "Games People Play." Not long after they'd passed by with their sweet song, we heard the rumbling of a stampede.

When people ran down the stairs in groups, it sounded like an angry herd of beasts. The feet slowed down and stopped on our floor. Ricky, Derrick, and Jon Jon rushed into the square, pretending to jump rope, mimicking our girlish mannerisms and singing rope songs they'd heard us belting out on the school playground. They were a little crew like us.

With the exception of Tonya, we were all in Ms. Pierce's class. At school, we had to be kind and respectful to each other, because Ms. Pierce made us act like a loving family, but back at the building, we pretended we couldn't stand one another; none of us really knew what to do with the actual affection that we felt. It seemed like a flaw to have these emotions. We didn't know then that the practice of burying emotions created adults who'd struggle to build meaningful relationships; some of us would eventually completely forget how to access true feelings. In my family, we expressed love in many ways, reaching out to touch an arm in a sad moment or smothering one another in a hug, but I knew, even from a very young age, that this behavior was rarely meant for people outdoors.

"Come on," Ricky said to Stacia, "turn it."

His face changed to serious as he concentrated, then rocked his chest back and forth, following one of the ropes. Stacia's arms flew out wider than they needed to, and she popped her hips while blowing these huge bubbles with her wad of Bubblicious gum.

"Just jump in," I said, laughing. Then he did it. Stacia and Tonya turned the rope around him. We were shocked at how he jumped in and skipped over the ropes like he did this all the time. Ricky was one of those kids who could play any sport you threw his way.

Tonya didn't know them, but she laughed with us, and I could tell she was enjoying herself. Ricky's boys, Derrick and Jon Jon, who were cousins, yelled and cheered for him and after the rope stopped, he jumped around the square, waving his hands up and down like he'd won an NBA championship. We each screamed something, cheering for Ricky or pretending to shoo him away.

In the middle of the noise, I saw Ricky and Tonya look at

each other. It was a quick moment, but long enough to embarrass her and to freeze the muscles on Stacia's face.

We all secretly had a crush on Ricky, but Stacia had verbally claimed him as her man.

"You want to go?" I asked Derrick, who was making fake jump shots toward Precious. They liked each other; their desks were side by side in school, and I'd seen them flirting. One time, Derrick even passed her a note asking, "Do you like me, check yes or no!" She'd balled it up and thrown it in her desk, but I saw these cute patches of red, like cartoon hearts, on her cheeks. We pretended to hate Ricky, Derrick, and Jon Jon but actually didn't mind that they put on too much cologne and ran around the square, their scent lingering there for hours.

"Nope," Derrick said.

"We out," Ricky announced, then stepped back and shot a fadeaway in my direction.

"Get that out of here!" I hollered, pretending to knock it out of the air. He rushed over and pushed me, then we all started shoving each other, play-fighting. Tonya scurried over to the corner, scared, so I said, "Mercy! Mercy!" our code word that made them stop. They laughed and ran down the stairs. We all caught our breath while looking at Tonya over in the corner. She trembled a little, her face serious.

"It's still Precious's turn," I said, and Stacia rolled her eyes. She had absolutely no tolerance for her unusual behavior. I handed Tonya the rope, and she walked over to the spot.

We eased into position and played a few more rounds, until without any warning, Stacia dropped the ropes and said, "I'm going to get a snow cone."

"I'm coming!" I said quickly, and Precious gave me a look so heavy with warning that I snapped, "You ain't nobody mama!"

She looked hurt and embarrassed, her face involuntarily contorting, then angry blushing. She spun around, her pigtails flying, and went toward her apartment.

We both knew the rules. While Stacia and Tonya roamed the building, Precious and I weren't supposed to leave the porch without an adult, but I was showing off in front of my new friend. Tonya followed me. Stacia and I ran down the stairs until we got to the last three, then holding on to the rail, we swung around to the next landing. I heard Tonya behind me, her feet hitting all the stairs, so I stopped and schooled her.

When we got to the first floor, I knew something wasn't right. Usually, when we walked out of the building, we had to weave through guys standing around, lining the brick wall that faced the entrance. They always looked so relaxed, like kids hanging out at a rec center, smoking cigarettes or weed and shooting dice. The parking lot was usually full of cars thumping bass that smothered the lyrics, so you couldn't really understand what the rapper said, but that day, it was quiet.

Maybe I could've ignored all these signs if I didn't see the gangbangers huddled up together getting instructions from their leader.

At the candy truck, we greeted Ms. Rose, this nice lady, old enough to be our grandmother. She'd packed up some of the candy, and I could tell, even though it was early evening, with hours of sun left, that she was about to leave. While I pointed to banana Now and Laters and Flamin' Hots, and gave her my flavor choices for a snow cone, I watched Tonya. She stood off to the side, looking at her shoes, kicking rocks around. This wasn't how you behaved when you were about to get some candy. You craned over those boxes, breathing in the yummy fruit flavors. Her body language told me that she didn't have any money.

I looked back at the building to see if Precious watched us from the window. I saw her lime-green tank top popping against white curtains.

What I'd said to her was mean, and I would apologize. I snapped on her because she was right; she was right most of the time, but that summer, I'd often choose fun over right.

I GOT TONYA A SNOW cone and gave her half of the other sweets. Stacia didn't like that I was sharing with her, so she yanked her body around and went to talk to her brother. He was standing a few feet away under a tree, scanning the parking lot and State Street. He wasn't a Lookout, but that day, everyone downstairs seemed to be more alert and tense.

"Roady, give me five dollars," I heard Stacia say. Me and Tonya hung back, standing in a space between the candy truck and where Stacia had gone. Roady puffed on a cigarette and didn't move. His little sister buzzed around him for a while, talking at him, but he stood there like a statue, his gaze fixed down the street. I didn't want to leave Stacia and Tonya, but everything in my body told me that something was about to happen and that I should go upstairs.

Roady tossed his cigarette behind him and pushed Stacia toward the building. He walked by me, and I saw a gun holstered on his hip. He turned around, still walking, and said, "Get yo' lil ass in the house, we in war."

He joined the huddle of dudes, and we broke for the building.

This is how we usually found out that the block was in war. Anybody could warn you: a wino, a store owner, a crackhead, a gangbanger. You would be minding your business, and somebody would say, "Better get in the house, we in war!"

Before we could make it into the building, we heard the shots. That huddle of guys cracked open and rushed in all directions, including ours. In the tunnel leading to the stairway, somebody had killed the lights, so it was hard to see in front of you, and though you could still hear the shots, they were muffled, since we were engulfed in brick and concrete.

I slipped on something and fell into the darkness, my pieces of candy and snow cone smacking me in the face as I hit the ground. Tonya tried to come back and help me, but this older dude named Nook told her, "Tonya, go!" while he lifted me off the ground and hurled my body toward the stairway. A flock of white tees caught up with us, and some dudes pushed us out of the way, while others jumped over us, the sounds of bullets motivating us all to keep going.

We ran hard up those few flights of stairs. On the third floor, I told Tonya and Stacia, "Come on!" and dragged them toward my door. We met Mama halfway down the porch. One by one, we ran into my apartment, then curved around the corner and hunched down in the hallway. My brother, Meechie, crouched at the living room window, his face pressed against the bars. Mama said, "Get out that damn window. You want to get shot?" His shoulders sagged, and he joined us in the hall. Mama examined us. "Everybody okay?" she asked, but reading her face, I could tell that she was suppressing panic at who I'd brought into our home: Tonya, some unkempt kid she'd probably never seen before, and a Buchanan.

When Stacia and I had become friends, we'd mostly played together outside. Mama wasn't a fan of the Buchanan family, but she never told me that I couldn't play with her. Once Stacia started coming to the square, Mama peeked out at us more often, just to make sure Stacia was on her best behavior.

We nodded our heads fast and panted, answering Mama's question, and sat shoulder to shoulder, knees pulled up to our chest, because the hallway was too skinny to stretch out our legs. Mama sat across from me and Tonya. She asked her, "What's your name?" but her voice echoed, and Tonya jumped. I saw her judging Tonya too, her eyes taking in dirty shorts, dusty gym shoes, filthy brown hair. I got so nervous, I tried to answer the questions for her.

"Her name's Tonya," I said. Mama shot me a look that said *Be quiet and let her talk.* Meechie looked bored. He picked at a hangnail for a while, then he rose up and walked away from us.

"Meechie!" Mama said, her voice tight.

"Bathroom," he said, with too much bass in his voice. We watched him until he disappeared. The shots seemed to stop, but we sat there listening to him pee, then flush the toilet and wash his hands. When the door opened, we all looked at him until he sat down again. Stacia shocked us all when she started talking to Meechie, like they were good friends.

"We in war with the Low End! I bet them Hooks came running down State Street, and we started bussing at them!"

"Stacia?" Mama said, horrified.

"Huh?"

"Honey, he doesn't need to hear this."

Meechie frowned at Mama, and Stacia's face went blank.

Mama turned to Tonya and asked, "What's your number? I want to call your mother and tell her you're okay."

"We ain't got no phone," she said.

I saw Mama's reaction to the word *ain't.* She cleaned up the wrinkles right away, though, and crawled into the kitchen to get the phone. I heard her leaving a voice mail for Gail, Stacia's mama.

Stacia's head snapped up, and she looked over at me and asked,

"How your mama know my number?" I hunched my shoulders, and curiosity wrinkled my face too.

Mama came back to the hallway and asked Tonya, "Won't she worry?" Tonya shook her head from side to side.

"Well, you can stay here until it's safe to go back out." Mama put both hands flat on the floor and pushed herself up. You couldn't call Mama fat, but she wasn't ever scrawny. I always thought she was just the size a mama ought to be. I remember those nights riding home from sightseeing downtown, and how I would lie on her soft arm while the bus took us back to the building. When I needed a hug, I'd get lost in the pillow of Mama's stomach.

From her standing position, she looked down at us and, using her slow, calm voice, said, "It's okay to go to your rooms, but stay on the floor." Then she walked down the hall. Meechie followed her, because he had to go in the same direction to get to his room. We joined the parade and filed into my room. "Stay on the floor," Mama said again.

It was summer, so there'd be the popping of both fireworks and gunshots on most days. We knew the difference between the two. Both made me a little jumpy, though neither fazed Meechie.

In my room, Tonya grabbed a Barbie doll, which I'd dismissed years prior, and Stacia reached for my favorite picture, the one of me and Meechie standing back-to-back. This was the first time either of them had come into my apartment, and they were treating my room like a store full of interesting artifacts.

"Who your brother go with?" she asked.

I snatched the picture from her, rolling my eyes. "I don't know. Nobody?"

She smiled, like she had a chance, then looked around the room, her eyes thirsty for information. When she landed on my journal, its pink-and-gold cover peeking out from under the bed skirt, I kicked it fully underneath the bed. She looked up at me for a moment, and though she didn't say anything, I could tell that she wanted to ask me about it.

It's possible she decided in that moment, she too wanted a place to keep all of her thoughts, a secret place where she could make sense of the feelings she wasn't encouraged to express out loud.

Concluding her tour from the floor, Stacia asked, with a nasty look on her face, "You want to be a teacher or something?" I retraced her steps, glancing at the globe, the maps on my wall, and my bookcase full of thick novels, before I raised and dropped my shoulders.

"You don't ever think about people in other places?"

"For what? We in the best place to be."

Tonya looked up from Barbie, her face asking Stacia's if she'd lost her mind. She dropped her head and mumbled something.

"Huh?" I said.

Then Tonya repeated herself and said, "I wanna go to Mississippi. Where my daddy at."

The crinkles in Stacia's forehead deepened, then she asked Tonya, "How you know Nook?"

I gave her my undivided attention then, because I wanted to know too.

"He live on my floor," Tonya told her, her eyes still on Barbie.

"On the ten?" Stacia asked.

Tonya nodded.

Then Stacia sang, in a snotty voice, "Tonya from the Ten. That's what we gone call you. I hope you don't think you the only Tonya in this building." She laughed a little, then told her, "Everybody got your name." I frowned at her. Tonya didn't seem to care, but I knew, even back then, that something about this nickname was an insult.

None of us had a close relationship with those other Tonyas. One of them was three years old, a younger sibling of our classmate. Another was some older lady who lived by herself, had no kids, and most people turned their noses up at because she kept to herself and wouldn't tell anyone her business. The third Tonya I could think of hung out in the playground with Stacia's older sisters, was some gangster's girl. I guess Tonya was just one of those names. All of those Tonyas were attractive, the last thing you wanted to be if you were a girl living in the hood.

I chose to believe what Tonya said, that Nook lived in an apartment on the tenth floor, that she knew him because he was her neighbor. The other option, that she—a twelve-year-old—had a personal relationship with this grown man, who was a drug dealer and gangster, was too much to handle.

After giving Tonya a new name, Stacia seemed proud of herself and done with us.

An awkward tightness swirled around. Before I could fix it, Stacia told us, "Y'all boring!" and hopped up and stomped out of the room and eventually the front door. We heard it slam. Mama ran into the hallway, and Meechie's door opened.

"Stacia left," I explained.

Mama said, "Okay." Then it was quiet again. I looked at Tonya sitting in the corner, stroking Barbie's hair. I sat down there next to her.

"You can have it, if you want."

She looked over at me and smiled, then nodded. I'd seen a glimpse of this smile a few times throughout the day, but in my room, holding that doll, it was strong, unfiltered, and it lingered for longer than a few seconds. I think that's the moment I decided that I wanted to make her smile as much as possible.

"You so nice," she said. Then *I* smiled. "How come you friends with Stacia?"

Before I could answer, Mama came into my room to give us a motivational speech. I always thought that Mama missed her calling as an educator. She reminded me so much of Ms. Pierce the way she was always correcting our grammar and uplifting everyone, but she used those skills as a homemaker, trying her best to raise two kids by herself in a war zone.

She grabbed me and Tonya into a hug, then said, "One day, you girls will get to live in a better place."

I moved my face from her chest and asked, "So we Lease Compliant?"

A new tension entered the room, and Mama snapped, "Where did you hear that term?"

"Downstairs" was all that I said before asking, "Are we?"

"You let me worry about that," she said, trying to walk away, stumbling a little. She couldn't leave my room fast enough. Those two words had spooked the whole block, even Mama.

THREE

Lease Compliant

In April of 1999, the Chicago Housing Authority started tearing down the buildings on our block. A year before that, near
the end of our fifth-grade school year—before Stacia and Tonya
were around—Precious and I sat in class and listened to Ms.
Pierce read an article from the *Chicago Tribune* about how they'd
started knocking down the buildings in the Hole, at the very
end of the State Street Corridor, one of the most notorious blocks
of Robert Taylor high-rises.

Sitting directly across from my building like its reflection,
4946 had been empty for months. Black boards replaced curtains,
and the porch lights stopped blinking on every night. Then, the
day came when the CHA began the slow, agonizing process of
knocking it down.

On that April afternoon, at 3:30 on the dot, Precious, Stacia,
and I burst out of the front doors of John Farren Elementary like
the building had caught fire, spilling onto 51st and State. Each
afternoon we performed this dramatic exit. If we landed on the
sidewalk and had the light, we could break all the way across

the street and down the block to the building, but on this day, we got stuck at the curb.

Precious stood poised, as if it were picture day, prepared for a photographer's shots, but Stacia jumped up and down screaming, "They fighting! They fighting!" because she could see a mob of people down by the buildings.

Her announcement hyped everybody up. Kids started pushing against the crossing guards, some of them no bigger than us, because they were just kids too. When the light turned green, me and Stacia threw our bodies hard against the wind. Since the very beginning of our friendship, we hadn't stopped racing, determined to prove that we were faster and stronger than the other. Precious tried her best, but she ran way behind us, even though she ate the healthiest foods and went to bed early like she was supposed to.

I knew why she couldn't keep up. She kept too many things in her book bag: nasty sugar-free snacks, books to read in the morning before school, books to read at lunch, lotions and sunscreen to keep her yellow skin unburned, and a change of shoes. As long as I'd known her, she'd been packing that stuff in her bag every day.

I heard her back there yelling, "Wait! Fe Fe!" but I couldn't slow down, not with Stacia challenging me to a race. Because I was faster than Stacia, I got to the building first. When I reached the playground, I saw what people were actually doing: nothing. They seemed frozen in place, looking up. There was a red construction vehicle reaching up to the top floor, swinging a ball into the structure. I looked over for Stacia, and only found Precious there. Stacia had skirted through the crowd and found her family. That summer, her allegiance would jump back and forth between us and them.

The Buchanans had always been drug dealers with the *Gangster Disciples*, called *GDs* for short, and *Folks* affectionately among one another. By the time they came to 4950, they had high rank within the GDs. Gail, the mother, chose our building so that her family's status and cash flow wouldn't change. Not all the high-rises were controlled by the same gang, so when she had to relocate, she was wise enough to select a building with the right affiliation. Since most of her kids were in and out of jail, they were no longer Lease Compliant, and CHA wouldn't give them a Section 8 voucher to leave the projects—only the option to choose another building. If you had a criminal record or didn't pay your rent consistently, you wouldn't be Lease Compliant, and you'd get shuffled around the projects until they were all gone. After the last projects were evacuated, some people squatted in the abandoned buildings or became homeless. The luckiest among this group moved in with family members in other troubled neighborhoods.

You could spot a Buchanan right away: they all had long, narrow heads and squinty eyes. Put that together with a face that could fold into these thick creases when they got confused or mad, and they looked a lot like bloodhounds to me. Gail had twelve kids, but by that school year, three of them didn't live in apartment 1502 with her. One of her sons, Chuck, was serving time in the penitentiary for murder, drugs, and gun possession, and Boo, a nine-year-old, was locked up too, tried as an adult because the police said he fit the description of a kid who pushed a seven-year-old out of a vacant apartment window. Ed left the family business before Stacia was even born. He was grown and lived with his wife and kids in Hammond, Indiana. She hadn't mentioned Ed that summer, the outcasted Buchanan. The other nine Buchanan kids lived in 1502, a four-bedroom apartment. The youngest ones—Peach, an eighth grader; Stacia in sixth; Moon, Ty, and Jet, third, first, and kindergarten—transferred from Beethoven to Farren and terrorized kids in the lunchroom and on the playground. One of her brothers, Sweat, was my brother's age. Later that summer, I'd develop a little crush on him.

On this day, the afternoon of 4946's demolition, her entire family gathered, a rare occurrence. In fact, everyone seemed to be on break from what they usually did on the block. Gangsters paused drug sales and just stared. Crackheads, winos, and little old ladies were there, looking too.

When I saw Mama Pearl—who wasn't actually my grandma, but acted like it—my mouth fell open. She was in her seventies and only ever snuck outside before sunup. By the time we left for school in the mornings, her new-penny-colored Buick would be missing from its spot across from DuSable High School.

Mama Pearl stared at the wrecking ball, but I could tell her mind had dipped off to the good old days, when the buildings were still infants and she was a young adult.

Before her hair turned white from stress or horror or just old age, Mama Pearl, whose real name is Lucille Perkins, worked with my grandma, Mabel Stevens, at the White Cake and Candy Company in Jackson, Mississippi. Mama Pearl got these plump fingers with wide nails, so I couldn't imagine them wrapping tiny foils over truffles. I learned over the years not to be surprised by anything this woman could do. Though they were surrounded by the scent of butter and chocolate and even tasted the sugar in the air, their lives in Mississippi were soured by hate crimes and poverty.

Most of the girls in the candy shop spent their shift gossiping, but Mama Pearl worked out her escape route. Outside the glass window, huge trains clanked and screeched, beckoning her. When they pulled into the station, just across from the shop, her fantasy of hopping aboard played out in her mind, and talk of boyfriends and church socials were tuned out. This was the plan: on her eighteenth birthday, she and Grandma would take that train north to Chicago, and Lucille's father would help them rent an apartment. Mama Pearl had no clue that she and Grandma were headed toward the original Candy Land. In 1944, only a week after their arrival at the Roosevelt station, they would both land jobs at the Curtiss Candy Company, the makers of Baby Ruth and Butterfinger.

Six months after their move north, Grandma got engaged to my grandfather, Percival Stevens. After the wedding, she and Mama Pearl lost touch. But Mama Pearl wasn't bitter or discouraged. Grandma left Curtiss Candy to be a homemaker, and Mama Pearl kept working. Eventually, she'd rent a room from a woman who owned a dry cleaner's at 43rd and State Street, just blocks away from where Grandma lived in the newly built Robert Taylor Homes. One day, she boarded the State Street bus, the same bus that Grandma was on, and they began chirping updates at one another. When Grandma told Mama Pearl about the Robert Taylor Homes, urging her to come to dinner that night, Mama Pearl agreed, and she fell in love with the community the complex provided.

Though the brick structures cast shadows on the block, the gardens and playground were lovely, and the neighbors helped keep an eye on one another's children. Mama Pearl left the dry cleaner's and moved onto the same floor as Grandma. She babysat Mama and my auntie Nora and became part of our family.

Over the years, she'd watched cute little kids grow up to become fiends or drink themselves to death, dying in their forties. She'd seen descendants of her friends ruin their family names, one generation at a time. For Mama Pearl, it wasn't just about the demolition of iron gates and bricks; what had already broken her heart was the destruction of so many families over the years.

We all looked up at the ball swinging from a metal cord, breaking apart the building's sharp angles. Some people watched and let their minds wander. Other folks stepped right up to the mic. Earl, who everybody dismissed as just a drunk, and his boy from back in the day, Woody, who got his name because his legs looked like wobbly mop sticks in a bucket of gym shoes, came to the front of the crowd and started a tag team elegy, spreading the odor of soured liquor across the crowd.

"Didn't I tell you?" Woody said, tapping Earl on the chest with the back of his hand. "I told you they was gone knock 'em down. Goddamned Mayor Daley."

Earl responded and said, almost to himself, "Papa put 'em up." He took a swig from their shared crunched-up paper bag, then finished his thought: "Junior knocked 'em down."

"This don't make no damned sense! They just gone put us out?" a lady asked, cutting in.

Then this dude told her, "Tootie, yo' ass going right down the street to another building. You *know* you ain't Lease Compliant."

She kissed her teeth, put a hand on her hip, and rolled her eyes at him. Just the mention of this term, *Lease Compliant*, agitated the crowd—it had the same effect on Mama when I asked her about it—and they all started talking at the same time.

In that moment out there with everyone fussing about whether the CHA would deem them Lease Compliant, I started to wonder what would happen to my family if we weren't given the approval to move. I didn't know what it meant, but I saw the change in people after those words entered the atmosphere. Moving meant leaving our block, where we knew the rules. I worried about my brother switching neighborhoods as a sixteen-year-old. In the nineties, dudes got shot all the time if someone threw up a gang sign and it didn't get returned, proving that they were in the same gang.

I looked up at our window and saw him there, Meechie, his blackish-brown skin striped by white child-safety bars. Mama wouldn't let him go anywhere, just down the porch to see one of his classmates or to Mama Pearl's apartment to help her around the house.

Some kid snapped me back to the crowd when he asked, "Why come they tearing up that building?"

Quan, Stacia's oldest brother, the leader of the gang on our block, squatted down to his level, put a big, strong paw on his tiny shoulder, and said, "Because white people want to be closer to their jobs, Lil Man." He held his position, and more questions lit up the kid's face, but Tootie came back.

"And we don't get no damn say?"

"What you gone say?" that same guy asked her. The crowd, busy laughing at how he treated her, didn't see her snatch Earl's paper bag. It had a bottle of Crown Royal in it. She cracked it over the guy's forehead, spraying glass everywhere. People cursed and moaned, and as everyone rushed forward, trying to get at Tootie, I started moving back toward the building.

Mama Pearl swept me out of the fray, her arms like the wide wings of an eagle, dragging me and Precious away from the mess. I scanned faces, trying to locate Stacia. When I found her, what I saw was disturbing: she stomped and kicked at the ground, her face twisted up ugly, Buchanan wrinkles matching her brother and sisters who huddled near her, attacking that lady for what she did.

In the elevator, we checked ourselves. Precious wasn't cut, just shook, her skin hot pink, breath puffing out in short gusts.

I had blood running down the side of my face. I could feel a trickle. Mama Pearl dug around her bag, but by the time she found some crumpled-up tissues, stained with cocoa flecks of powdered foundation, the scent of a tiny alcohol pad filled the metal square. Precious handed me the wet, stiff wipe, then a Band-Aid strip. Mama Pearl stuffed her tissues back into her purse. You could hear the eerie groaning of elevator cords until the doors opened on the third floor. We rushed off, but I froze when Mama Pearl called my name.

She told me, "Stop running with that Buchanan child, trying to save her."

Mama Pearl knew me well. She'd been in my life since the day that I was born. After my grandmother passed away, she'd taken over the job, loving on me and Meechie, trying to mold us into something positive. Since Mama had no doubt told her about my friendship with Stacia, she'd been watching me even closer.

"What you gone do with *your* life? Huh? That's what you needs to be thinking about." She started walking, but I stood there, watching her. The words hanging back with me. I hadn't thought about what I wanted to do with my life just yet, only what I would do after school every day. The answer was usually the same: grab my friends, jump rope.

I waved slowly at Precious, who lived on the same end of the floor as Mama Pearl, then walked the other way, toward my apartment. I stopped at the iron, crisscrossed gate—our window out into the neighborhood—and jammed my face against it. I could see that the crowd had begun to spread out and return to its usual activities. I scanned the playground for Stacia, and worried when I didn't see her anywhere. Then she appeared next to me. We looked through the gate, quiet. I stared at the woman on the ground, lying in the place where we once stood.

She wasn't moving.

"You think she dead?" I asked. When Stacia didn't reply, I moved my face from the gate. She didn't move hers. I put mine back and asked myself, *Did my friend just help kill somebody?* It was strange to think about. Though we dropped the topic then, I would return to this moment later in the summer, and throughout the years.

That day, the wrecking ball broke apart the bricks and window frames, never stopping, even when the crowd got crazy. Even though somebody lay motionless on the ground. Broken parts of the building fell out of the sky, slow, feather-like; it hypnotized us, and we all sat like that, watching, for a while. Then people remembered that they had jobs to do: help their kids with homework, sell drugs, start dinner, look for pop cans, beg for crack quarters—hoping they could collect enough change to buy rocks.

I moved my face from the iron gate, then Stacia peeled hers off. The building had branded us, the pattern of diamonds printed across our faces. We hung out for a bit, talking about the wrecking ball and updates on our crushes. Then we got back to what we usually did after school—grabbed the rope and started a game, going on with our lives. It wasn't long before the gate's imprint faded, but sometimes, when Stacia screwed her face up, and looked like her brothers and sisters, I thought about how that lady was dead, and that Stacia had helped stomp her to death.

That day is cemented in my memory. We watched them knock down what we thought was indestructible. I'd learn that so many things that I thought were solid and structured in my life could be broken down, bit by bit, just like those buildings.

FOUR

Tonya from the Ten

The shooting had stopped completely, and things were still and quiet downstairs, so we migrated to the kitchen table for dinner. Mama had composed herself after stumbling out of my room, running from my question about being Lease Compliant. She'd started cooking; the motions of preparing meals and the fragrant scents of herbs always soothed her.

Tonya was invited to stay. She ate Mama's cooking like it was her last meal. Mama kept looking over at her, but Tonya didn't notice with her back arched over her plate in holy communion with the peas; she almost got mashed potatoes on her nose. Mama couldn't take it for too long, and eventually said, "Tonya, baby, slow down before you choke."

Tonya acknowledged the words by cutting her eyes over at Mama, then chewed slower but never really sat up straight like the rest of us. Meechie ate like this sometimes. What Mama usually said to him was "Boy, you are *not* an animal. Stop shoveling food into your mouth like it's trying to get away," but she gave Tonya a voice dripping with honey. We sat at the table, the four of us too quiet, though inside I was cursing Mama out about how she wouldn't answer my question about moving.

I stared out the kitchen window into the playground. I didn't even see a nervous cat trotting around. No teenagers leaning on sliding boards, caking. No angry words hugged by bass, sending vibrations throughout the parking lot and upstairs into our windows. A car or two zipped down State Street, the drivers from other neighborhoods, unaware of the war, but no doubt concerned that they were driving by the projects with no streetlights. We knew who caused that blackout, just didn't know *how* the gangbangers turned out the lights.

With both Meechie and Tonya concentrating on their food, it was like me and Mama were the only people at the table. I caught her eyes more than once, and since I kept thinking about whether we were Lease Compliant, and how Mama could just tell me so I wouldn't have to worry, I'm sure I sent some snotty looks her way.

She finally said, "Felicia, we're not going to talk about it."

Before she even finished her sentence, I rolled my eyes. Mama put her fork down with so much force that both Meechie and Tonya jumped. Her body leaned forward in my direction with her head tilted, as if to ask me if I'd lost my little mind. Meechie and Tonya looked at me. It was my move. I backed down.

"Okay," I said.

"Okay?"

I was calm when I told her, "We don't have to talk about it." Meechie looked at me with a confused smile, then at Mama with the same face, and shook his head a little. Then he dismissed us entirely and went back to his food. He'd started treating me and Mama like we annoyed him, making these faces with a hint of disgust, like we were children, and he was *such* an adult who had risen well above the pettiness that women and girls got into. He wouldn't even go downtown with us anymore, deciding instead to stay home, alone. It had hurt my feelings, this intentional distance. I could feel him growing up and away. At least, that's what I thought was happening. Years later, I'd learn that he had been dealing with violent attacks from the gang in an attempt to get him to join them, and that going downtown to see Chicago landmarks was the last thing on his mind.

Mama picked up her fork and moved on, but I didn't leave the moment. I sat there, thinking about all the ways that I could find my own answers to the things that my family wouldn't tell me. The easiest way? Stacia. She sat on a hill of knowledge about everything Mama tried to keep from me. I would get all the information I wanted, but it wouldn't stop there; that summer, I'd pull back the curtain and see all the grime hiding in our neighborhood, and I would be sorry that I ever went looking for it.

Right after dinner, Mama told Tonya that it was time for me to get ready for bed. She asked her, "Where do you live?"

"On the ten."

"Say the tenth floor," Mama said.

In the square, we all said "on the ten," even Precious, who was nearly a pastor's kid. I just flipped back and forth to cut down on lectures. Tonya repeated what Mama said, then we left to take her home. We walked down the dark hall using years of familiarity to guide us. It was especially eerie with no sound. Through the gate, staring at us, you could make out traces of 4946, the side where the wrecking ball had started crushing it only two months before barely visible. While it was difficult to see the building clearly with no lights downstairs, we could feel it out there in the darkness, the wind whipping the caution tape wrapped around its opening. I stared over there and something strange happened:

I saw a flash of light. I blinked my eyes a few times, thinking I was seeing things, then it happened again, this time four flashes.

People had been moving out of there all school year, leaving Farren in chunks. New kids got dumped into our school from the other projects that hadn't closed yet. Now 4946 looked like a haunted house, about three floors busted wide-open. We walked to the elevator, which was powered by a generator, and it came right away. When the door opened, we squinted at the bright light inside. On the tenth floor, Tonya spun around and said, "I'm okay," like Mama would let her walk to her apartment in the dark, alone. Mama nudged us off the elevator, and said, "Come on."

She lived in our exact apartment. We stayed in 310, she was in 1010. I was so excited to meet her mama, and to see what her apartment looked like, because I figured her mama would invite us in and talk to Mama. I bounced down the porch, not paying any attention to Tonya's body language. She walked quick, like she'd outrun us. At the door, she hadn't even turned the key in the lock before it swung open. It was her mama, Rochelle.

"Hell you been?" she hollered at Tonya, who squirmed past her, mumbling, "On the three." I looked right at Mama, daring her to correct Tonya now.

She jumped in, the fingertips of her right hand pressing hard against her sternum. "I'm Janice. Tonya was downstairs on the third floor playing rope with my daughter and two other girls. I took her in when the shooting started. I wanted to call, but you don't have a phone?" Mama said, pretending it was a question.

Rochelle said, "Naw, ain't no damned phone."

I was all in her business. This is what I remember: Four missing teeth, one from the top front, three gone at the bottom. A face that looked like she'd been in a few fights with wild cats, the animals taking chunks of her skin with them. And what she wore, a tube top that hugged her rib cage and left her belly exposed, looked like it used to belong to Tonya—when she was much younger.

They didn't have much furniture. The living room was empty, like a dance floor at the start of a party. The kitchen had this tiny wooden table that didn't match the three chairs. The fake leather on the chairs was cracked and peeling, cotton popping its head out of the rips. The windows had dingy, holey curtains. My eyes hit blank wall after blank wall and bounced onto the floor, then up the table legs of that rickety table.

My view got cut off when the door started moving without door-closing language. I heard Rochelle say, "Alright," but didn't think that would be the last thing. I was used to adults saying too many words and things they didn't really mean to people they didn't even like, but this lady, like Mama Pearl and Ms. Pierce, said exactly what she felt, and no more than she needed to.

I planned to tap Tonya for last tag or wave bye, but Rochelle didn't care about any of our kid rituals. Tonya didn't smile at me. All I saw was shame for everything we'd just witnessed. Mama and I walked down Tonya's porch in silence. I looked over at 4946 and the playground and what little equipment remained—the frame of the swing set and a dented sliding board—looked like dollhouse furniture from ten stories up. I was troubled by what had just happened. I guess Mama felt the same, because she hit me with a million questions. In the elevator, before the door could even close, she asked me, "How did you meet Tonya?"

"She walks by the third floor all the time. Today I asked her if she wanted to play rope." Mama smiled at me. It made me blush, which was more of a feeling than a physical color change because I'm not fair-skinned like Precious. I smiled back.

"What do you know about her mother?"

"Nothing," I said, but that was actually a lie. I suspected that her mother was a crackhead, because the moment she yanked her door open, I recognized her face: Rochelle was in the crowd that gathered to watch the demolition that day. Instead of looking up at her childhood building and fussing like everybody else, she was two-stepping and scratching, and every once in a while, she whispered something to a gangbanger. She moved around the crowd doing this, and though the gangbangers acknowledged her, they all seemed to brush her off, irritated. It was like she wasn't even in the crowd for the same reasons we were. She was on another mission.

Mama continued her interrogation all the way home. "Does she have brothers and sisters?" I hunched my shoulders. Mama just looked at me for a few seconds, then asked, "Something wrong with your mouth?"

"She didn't say."

"Barely said anything."

"She used to live in 4946," I told her, happy to come up with something.

"So they were relocated." She nodded, going off on her own thoughts. The minute we got in the house, Mama said, "She needs to comb her hair and get some clothes that fit. She always look like that?"

"Yes," I told her.

"Ask her if she likes your braids. Tell her to ask her mother if I can do her hair on Sunday."

"Okay," I said. She walked to her room, and I watched her until she was gone.

My mama took parenting seriously. It was her full-time job. Her mother instilled this in her and encouraged her to stay home and raise her children because you couldn't trust other people with your babies. Mama would spend her days prepping our meals, cleaning the house, and even popping in on us at school. I don't remember her going off to work until much later in life; I was in high school when she started working at a hotel, cleaning rooms while taking classes at a community college. I couldn't imagine how miserable Tonya's life had to be with Rochelle for a mother. I'd find out, though.

IN BED THAT NIGHT, I couldn't stop thinking about Rochelle. I wondered what it was like to have a crackhead for a mother, and then eventually my thoughts drifted over to Stacia. I hoped she would warm up to Tonya. That's when I first asked myself, *Did I make a mistake bringing this girl around? Will she be worth all the trouble?*

I drifted off to sleep with visions of Rochelle bopping in that crowd to music that no one else could hear, scratching her face while her old building fell to pieces.

FIVE

Summer School

The next day, even though it was summer, and I wasn't required to, I popped up and got ready to go to school. I went down the porch to grab Precious, who also had the grades to skip summer school, but had parents who wouldn't let her, and we walked over together. Stacia *had* to go to summer school; it was the only way she'd pass to the seventh grade.

This had been our routine for years: Mama would watch me walk down the long hall to go pick up Precious. I'd go inside and wait on her couch covered in protective plastic. Her mama would greet me with a big smile, calling me by my whole first name, Felicia—the Browns weren't big on nicknames—then we'd trot off to school. It had been this way since we were ten, and walking to school on our own. This year especially, summer school was good for us. We had time away from the constant crumbling of the building—both inside and out.

As soon as we popped out of the building's opening, we could see the kids over across the street on the school grounds, and our hearts twirled at the joy to come. It's the same feeling we'd experience on field trip day, when the school buses drove up to Six Flags Great America, and the roller coasters seemed to grow all around the bus as we approached the entrance of the amusement park.

It was a massive, wobbly rope, going around seven sweaty girls wildly kicking limbs, dressed in summer outfits, posing, with mouths open, smiles stretched to capacity. We could hear two girls belting out that song that we both knew so well. That was the main stage. In the background, a tiny army of boys ran from one end of the playground to the other, playing their favorite game, Run G Run, which looked a lot like soccer, now that I think of it, but there was never a ball. We noticed them, but they weren't our whole world—more like sprinkles on top of the sweet and simple life we had.

The girls turning the rope over all those jumping bodies worked so hard. They whipped a single wire coated in plastic over that line of kids fast, and on beat, as they sang that song:

> *All in together, any kinda weather*
> *I see teachers*
> *looking out the window*
> *Ding, dong, the fire bell*

By the time we reached the rope, three girls had jumped out, and there was space in the rope for more kids, so we jumped in. Not long after we were in the rope, some other kids joined us. I recognized that cologne; it was Ricky, Derrick, and little Jon Jon, who wasn't in our grade, because he was two years younger. I could still see the other boys running back and forth, playing their game, but Ricky and his crew wanted to come and be close to us.

If they weren't the right boys crashing our game—the cute,

cool, confident ones—the girls turning would stop and shoo them away, their faces tight with wrinkles of disgust. But since we all had crushes on these two boys, and little Jon Jon was adorable, we allowed the intrusion, and the girls on the end turned harder, and we jumped with even more exaggeration.

The game continued, and the song restarted while they yanked the rope to the beat. We were always amazed to see the boys playing what everyone believed to be a girls' game. It never occurred to us that this wasn't so special, that boys could jump up and down over a rope and girls could catch a football and run with it or simply run away when they heard someone yell, "Run, G, run!"

By the time Stacia marched onto the grounds, we were tired of playing All. We had a little time before the first bell rang, and we had to bolt to our spots in front of the doors to wait for Ms. Pierce, so I whispered to Precious and Stacia, "Let's run with the boys!"

They both looked at me with wide eyes, then Stacia took off running, even though we didn't have a plan, and we didn't really know anything about why they were running up and down the playground. But that was how she was: a rocket, full of fire.

The group engulfed her, and even though we couldn't see her, we knew that she was in there, so when the boys ran back our way, we joined them. We didn't know who was "it" or how you won the game, but we ran with them, and when some of the boys frowned, and were confused about why we were in their game, we ran faster, cracking up. Ricky and Derrick yelled for us to go back to our girl games, but we just kept laughing and enjoyed the strange sensation of being engulfed in a sea of boys who we weren't afraid of. They were our classmates and our friends' brothers. They were familiar and safe, and at peace too. Back at the building, they had to hold their breath as they passed by the older boys who were making plans for their lives or who had caused unnecessary conflict with them, but for the most part, at school, when the day was young and playground monitors stood guard, we felt safe to be kids.

For the rest of summer school, whenever we felt like it, we crashed Run G Run. More girls joined us too. Some of the boys didn't like it, and wanted us to stay in our place, but you couldn't convince us that we had a place, so we did what we wanted whether they liked it or not. And our guys, who were not really our boyfriends, but something like that, they liked running with us—even though they'd never admit it.

When the second bell rang, we ran to our spots. Most teachers were already at the front of their lines, but Ms. Pierce loved to make an entrance. The door eased open, and she sashayed over to us, a can of Pepsi clamped in red manicured fingers. She never had much hair, and behind her back, Stacia called her "that baldheaded heifer" but never to her face and never anything harsher. Stacia had deep affection and respect for Ms. Pierce, and though she wouldn't have admitted it back then, she actually thought of her as a mother figure.

Our elementary school was not only a refuge in a season of life when we needed to take cover, but it also gave us an example—early in life—of how influential an educator could be. Ms. Pierce would raise the bar high for us, and my friends and I would all grow up expecting that level of quality and attentiveness from every teacher we encountered.

SIX

Sweeps

That evening, in bed, I stared at the ceiling thinking about how much fun I had running with the boys and drifted into sleep knowing I'd do it again, even if they pushed us and tried to send us back to the girl side of the playground. It would've been such a soft and lovely ending to a nice summer day, but then I heard the sounds. First, just two pops, then several—people were shooting in the playground again.

We lived three stories up, but somehow, on yet another night of gunslinging, a bullet found its way into one of our window frames. I flipped onto the floor and heard Mama call to check that we were okay. I yelled back, but Meechie was a deep sleeper. I heard Mama push open his door so hard that the knob banged against the wall. When she closed it, I knew that he was okay.

Those gunshots summoned a predator that seemed to hunt the entire neighborhood constantly. When the block was in war, you had to first evade flying bullets. Then, if you were still alive, it wouldn't be long before the cops showed up.

In 1988, they called it Operation Clean Sweep. It was the

brainchild of the CEO of the CHA at the time, and the sweeps were conducted by CHA security guards and Chicago Police. They pretended to have the tenants' best interests in mind, sweeping the buildings, looking for wanted criminals and weapons. They did not bring warrants. They just pounded on the door, and if tenants didn't comply with these inspections, they could be evicted.

Mama was young, in her twenties, and me and Meechie were so small back then; I was a year old and Meechie just four. These men would knock aggressively, and Mama would open it, and half of them would rip through our place, searching. The others barked leading questions like "You've got a man staying here who's not on the lease?" or "Where are the drugs?" and my young mom, alone in her apartment, terrified because it was now full of strangers yelling at her, sometimes with dogs, would plead with them while we cried, sensing danger from her reaction and the violent noise coming from sometimes seven different intruders.

The sweeps used to be random searches orchestrated by the CHA, but by the summer of 1999, the cops were in charge, and they decided when to sweep and who to lock up. They didn't pretend to search for fugitives or act on behalf of the CHA. They came to our door, and Mama, still afraid that noncompliance meant eviction, always opened it.

As a kid, I didn't know that Mama was scared we'd get put out. In her mind, we had nothing to hide, and it would be over before we knew it. What she didn't realize was that things were changing, that me and Meechie were growing up, and though she looked at us and saw her babies who couldn't harm anyone, the cops looked at Meechie and saw a gun-toting, drug-slinging criminal.

Mama rushed by my door, a blur of pink terrycloth. I swung out of bed and ran after her. In our hallway, I could hear more voices down the porch; it was so loud, it sounded like the neighborhood in the middle of the day. Flashlights cut through our living room window from the porch. There had to be ten or eleven of them on our end of the floor, banging on doors. Meechie hadn't left his bed and was still asleep. Mama hurried to the door, as if she'd left a good friend waiting too long.

"Mama, don't," I said, talking to her back. She didn't say anything, just kept moving, an obedient citizen. "Stacia said they can't come in without a warrant."

But Mama, used to opening the door during these sweeps, did what they wanted and let them in. It hadn't occurred to her that her son was now sixteen, and that the police might accuse him of being a gangbanger. She saw her sweet, curious boy and didn't view him through their lens.

Meechie wasn't a gangbanger, but even I knew he might be mistaken for one by the police, so I ran to the door to stop her, but it was too late. I put my hand over hers, already touching the knob. We got knocked back into the stove as they pushed into our space, fast and loud, an el train of law enforcement.

Combat boots dragged the outside into our kitchen, streaking the bleached-white tile with muddy crumbs from the stairway. Two of them stomped into the living room and dirtied up the thick rugs reaching out from under the couch. They jogged through the tunnel of our hallway, the only place we're safe when there's shooting. We ran after them, watching them kick open doors, going in our rooms, flipping over our mattresses and looking under the beds. They behaved as if they were hot on the trail of a fugitive they'd watched run into our apartment. One of them went in my room, his hip knocking over my globe as soon as he walked in, cracking the Earth.

His searching fingers raked my books onto the floor as if he'd find something illegal between the pages of my novels. I didn't have a voice to tell him to get out, this grown, white man in my room, in the middle of the night. I had on nothing, really, a T-shirt that barely covered my thighs. He wore an entire uniform with a cap and stars and a gun.

His skin, his clothes, his behavior in our apartment—I just kept thinking he didn't belong. I could hear Meechie's voice pleading, all high-pitched, then coughing. Me and the officer destroying my room bolted for the door. One of us knocked over the photo of me and Meechie, fracturing the glass. Then he yelled at me to "Stay here!" and went to Meechie's room too.

"Meechie!"

Mama howled his name over and over from outside his door. Then a police officer appeared at the end of the hall, because apparently one of them stayed by the apartment entrance. He walked down the hall from the kitchen, in no hurry, and said, "Ma'am, won't you come on in here, and sit down." It wasn't a question at all. He motioned for us to follow him down the hall. When we didn't move, he hollered, "Let's go!"

"Meechie!" Mama yelled at his door. "Mama's here!" Then she grabbed my hand, and we did what he said and sat on the couch. It was true. She was *here*, and he was *there*. And that's how it had been for a long time. She was *here*, and he was *there*. In his own world of gangster rap and whatever else he did in his room behind that closed door. We went downtown, and he was back at the building, in the apartment by himself. We visited Mama Pearl and he stayed home, alone, watching TV. We were always *here* while Meechie was *there*. It was his choice to stay back. That night, I felt all the times that we were separated, and I blamed Mama. If she hadn't opened the door, he would still be asleep. If she hadn't opened the door, their loud, dirty boots would've remained outside, and not in our sacred space, all over our peaceful, clean apartment. If she hadn't opened the door, my brother wouldn't have had the law choking him in his own bedroom.

THEY ALL CAME BACK TO the living room in a straight line, Meechie's face still smashed flat with sleep. I could see lines where the pillowcase creased marks into his jaw. He had dried saliva at the corner of his mouth, and everything else he had control over stretched into panic.

"Where you taking my boy?" Mama kept asking, her body stiff and straight, her hands reaching for him, but missing. They ignored her and walked him through the kitchen, going out the door. She kept asking it, over and over, running down the porch. It was the first time I ever saw Mama act like this. Lost. The porch was so dark, I could barely see any of them out there, but I leaned out the door anyway, and looked.

"You know where, Wentworth Precinct," one of them yelled. Then I couldn't hear them anymore as they took my brother farther and farther away. Just the slap of Mama's feet, walking slowly back to our wrecked home.

SEVEN

Makeovers

The precinct at 51st and Wentworth sits kitty-corner to the highway, so Meechie and I had passed it every time Uncle Tim drove us to his house in Roseland. That corner was our portal to a fantasy land, where people lived in houses, and there were no gunshots. In the squad car, I bet Meechie thought about Uncle Tim and longed for an escape up that highway. We had driven past that drab stone building a million times and had never been inside. We knew that it was a police station, and sometimes saw cops walking boys through the entrance in handcuffs, but that wasn't our life.

That night, he went to jail because he was Black and a boy, and to the police, that fit the description of a criminal. I'd learn that Black kids didn't get the luxury of appearing childlike and innocent, that from the moment we are born, some people start a clock on how long it'll take the boys to commit a crime, the girls to seduce.

I thought it would be obvious to the police that we were just a family, that we had nothing to do with the gang violence and drug culture swirling around us. Couldn't they tell that there was peace in our apartment? The walls in our house were covered with pictures of our family and a Jesus clock. We weren't pretending that people didn't get beat up or shot in the playground. What went on in our apartment was our business, and what they did downstairs was theirs. I would learn though, real quick, that we were all the same in the eyes of the law.

The Black kids who hadn't started committing crimes would eventually, the police believed, so taking them to jail, even if they hadn't done anything, was justified. This is how Meechie entered the system and began to ingest the idea that he had no options, that decisions about his life were not his to make: the gang had his future picked out for him; the police had plans too.

I think back to Meechie's days of whistling and playing with action figures, and I wonder how things would've been different if someone asked him what he wanted. If someone demanded he make some choices for himself, the way Mama Pearl did for me that summer. Maybe the worst part about growing up in public housing is that people think your body is public too. That even before you are born, your Black body already belongs to the owners of the land. That night, Meechie spent about two hours in jail, and that's all it took to cement his identity.

MINUTES AFTER THE RAID, WE were dressed and out in the darkness, headed to get my brother back.

A high steel counter hit us in the face once inside the police station. Immediately I felt as if I had entered an alternate universe. It was too cold for living bodies, like we were in Moo & Oink, a meat locker of a grocery store where Mama used to shop. Moo & Oink sold meat wholesale and froze me to the bone every time we went there. Maybe that's why the police at the station wore so much clothing. They had on the same things as the police who swept our apartment. At the station, where it was freezing and there was paperwork and staplers, shirts with collars, pockets, that metal star and stiff hat, it made sense.

I'd later learn about the appearance of power.

"Name?" the man at the counter asked Mama.

"Janice Stevens."

The man just shook his head from side to side, blinking all slow, and blowing out a puff of air like he had a headache and we were making it worse. "*Son's* name?"

"Demetrius Stevens," Mama said, then looked at me and said, "Go sit down."

I sat on a cold chair against the wall and watched her standing there filling out papers until one of the police pointed and said, "Over there."

When Mama came over, and sat next to me, I didn't look at her right away. While she had her head low, I snuck a peek. She wasn't wearing her Ebony Fashion Fair pressed powder, and she looked saggy all over; her expression made her face seem droopy, her shoulders slumped down, and she wasn't even wearing a bra.

The confident, teaching Mama that I had to put up with all day was back at the house. This was a woman I didn't recognize, a subordinate, frightened being. That night, nothing she said to the police mattered. She had no authority there, or even in her own home. The police talked to her like she was a child. They yelled at her, barked orders in half sentences, something she'd never let us get away with. They'd taken her son right out from under her. I had never seen such a disruption of power. I didn't know what they'd done to my mother and couldn't imagine what was happening to my brother while he was out of our care.

We waited, and I watched the men sitting behind the counter. They joked around with each other, and I wondered how they would like it if someone busted up their sleep, waking up their cop babies. I wondered if these guys had gone out on sweeps in the past, breaking up warm, cozy homes and dragging innocent, sleeping boys out of their beds in the middle of the night. This behavior, bursting into someone's home and dragging them away, is how lynchings were conducted. There had to be so much terror running through Mama's mind that night, knowing that other family members, Grandma's brothers and uncles, left the house in this same way, some never found, others found swinging from trees or in pieces in a river.

We sat in cold plastic chairs, shoulders trembling, teeth chattering. Since it was our first time in the station, it hadn't occurred to Mama that we would need jackets in the middle of the summer blaze. I will remember this incident when I am old enough to vote and someone plays a cruel joke on me, making this very station my polling place. I will travel by train from a theological seminary in Michigan to this police station right off the highway. The projects will be long gone by then. I will vote for Barack Obama with hope in my chest, but terrible thoughts of this night in my head. I will remember how cold the police station was, and I will bring a jacket.

Eventually, two figures appeared at the end of a long hallway. I stared down what seemed like a city block away, and finally, Meechie's lithe body, rocking from side to side, came into view. A police officer, in that same uniform, walked with him. I didn't know the look on my brother's face. The lines in his forehead were deep, like Buchanan wrinkles. The officer escorting him didn't have any special emotion on his face, just acted like he could've been pushing a shopping cart around Jewel, instead of walking my brother from a jail cell.

Mama hugged Meechie. His face cracked for a quick second, then he seemed to suck it back in place; he was about to cry but didn't. The whole thing made me weep instantly: the police busting in, the waiting, the freezing, my brother, out of the house, and in a cell? He broke free from Mama and wrapped his arm around the back of my neck. He smelled like some strong mustard greens, but I could smell a tiny hint of his Cool Water cologne.

"Stop crying," he told me. It was bossy, but I knew it was his best attempt to console me.

Mama tapped us a little, and said, "Come on."

It was about four in the morning by then, and still dark outside. I just knew that Mama would question Meechie about the whole thing. I planned to sit quietly and take in all the details. When we got home, though, she made us soup and grilled cheese sandwiches and Meechie mumbled, "Thanks, Ma," then went to his room and closed the door. Mama just stared at the place where the kitchen and the hallway met, all dumbfounded. That was the first sign that *our* Meechie never made it back home. Mama decided to leave him alone and give him some time to get back to what she thought could be normal again.

I ate my food, then got up, doing a fake pee dance. I went to Meechie's room, not the bathroom. The door was closed, but I could hear him moving around in there. He wasn't the type to talk out his feelings, but I eased his door open anyway. I stopped when I saw what he was doing. He had his headphones on his ears, but they were blasting so loud that I could hear the music. Shirtless, he punched at the air with tight fists while rapping:

Have that red shit pouring out your hair
Nigga, any-fucking-time, nigga, any-fucking-where

I would've been horrified to hear the words alone come out of his mouth, but paired with his Raiders cap banged to the side and pants sagging under his boxers, he looked just like the dudes downstairs, and that gave me a chill. He jumped around his room, throwing jabs at Michael Jordan's face, the Sox caps on the wall, his neon crossing guard belt from elementary school on his dresser. I couldn't decide whose right then and there, but this makeover was somebody's fault. I eased the door closed and tried to act normal when I returned to the kitchen with Mama. Meechie had begun a sort of metamorphosis, and though I'd regret not telling Mama about it, back then, my allegiance was to him. He was my brother, and I didn't want to do anything to get him into *more* trouble.

LATER THAT MORNING, WE ALL got up again and tried to jump back into our regular routines. Mama dragged a chair over to the stove, flipped on the burner, dropped the pressing comb in the fire, and turned on the radio. She couldn't clean the house or do my hair without playing dusties, so we welcomed Herb Kent into our home, a humorous DJ who was always picking fights with his cohost during the Battle of the Best on V103.

I sat on the cold kitchen floor, locked between Mama's thighs, flinching and holding my breath every time the pressing comb got close to my ear. The heat rose up stronger and stronger, like voices in a choir at a song's climax. I hated getting my hair done but loved the finished product. Two hours later, it was washed, detangled, dried, oiled, then cornrowed for the week.

When Meechie got out of bed and came in the kitchen looking for food, we stopped what we were doing and held our breath. "I'm cool," he said, and laughed a little. He made his food, and we tried to carry on, but that morning, it was so obvious that he wasn't a part of our little group, that me and Mama had so many rituals and inside jokes and moments that Meechie didn't have. He and Mama loved one another, but as he got older, I doubt that Meechie had anyone to go deep with. Since we couldn't relate to his experience of being assaulted by the police, and being locked up, Meechie stepped farther away from us. It was subtle, but I could feel it.

Tonya knocked on the door while Meechie was still in the kitchen. I let her in, and she said hi to everyone. With our attention on her, Meechie slipped out of the kitchen. I was excited to show Tonya the clothes that Mama set aside for her. Some of them were Mama's clothes that she had taken in on the sewing machine, sundresses and shorts mostly, and the other outfits were from Goodwill, where Mama bought a lot of our clothes.

Mama gave Tonya a little bag with soap, deodorant, and scented lotions in it. It came with a lecture about hygiene and how we were both young ladies who would be women before we knew it, and that we had to stay neat and groomed. I knew this talk was for Tonya, but Mama didn't want to make her feel bad. Mama had planned this makeover the moment she saw Tonya. What we didn't realize at the time was that the last thing that Tonya needed was any reason for people to pay *more* attention to her.

With new clothes and clean, braided hair, she looked even prettier than before. I asked Mama if she would braid Stacia's hair too. I told her that no one was nice to her, and that I thought that Stacia was so mean because she was a kid dealing with a lot of pain, that she tried to act tough, but she really didn't have a lot of people in her life who showed her love and affection. I thought that perhaps some kindness might warm Stacia's heart a bit and change her behavior. Mama listened, and I saw her face sliding from a straight-up *No* to a *Maybe*.

Tonya frowned; she wasn't convinced.

WHILE TONYA TOOK HER NEW stuff home, I went to grab Precious. We detangled the ropes in preparation for Tonya's return and Stacia's arrival.

I told Precious what happened to Meechie. We stood about a foot away from each other, pulling at the dirty bundle of strings. "They just took him out of his bed?" she asked, looking so concerned that I thought she'd cry. I nodded.

"It was so many of them," I said. "They pushed in the door and just came in, spreading out everywhere, looking through our stuff. Then they *all* went in Meechie's room, and he started coughing like somebody had choked him."

"I bet he was scared for his life," she said.

"He was!"

Even though it had happened already, and Meechie was home safe, Precious still looked terrified. "He okay?" she asked.

I hunched my shoulders. The truth was that he wasn't doing well, but I didn't want to admit it. He hadn't talked much in the house, and I'd never forget seeing him in his room singing that song about killing somebody. We continued pulling at the rope, undoing loops of knots in silence. I was still thinking about Meechie dressed like a gangster, and I'd later find out that Precious, who had no brothers, was thinking about how awful it would be if someone came into her house and treated her dad like that.

———

WE GOT TIRED OF WAITING for Tonya and Stacia, so Precious turned the rope around us the way we used to do when we were five-year-olds and had no other friends in the building. We jumped like that for a while, then Stacia rushed into the square, a bundle of energy.

I told Stacia what happened to Meechie, and her reaction was totally different. She didn't even stop chewing her Bubblicious when she told me, "Ain't like they could keep him in jail," as if the trauma of the experience weren't damaging enough. It was true, Meechie *was* back home, but before I could tell her about all the things they'd done to him in our house, she launched into a story.

"He at that age, Fe Fe. Everybody checking for him now. My brother left last year when he turned fifteen." I looked for a sadness, any crack at all in her hard shell, but she just reached for the ropes, motioning for us to start a game.

"Me and Sweat used to be close like you and Meechie. He'd read to me, Moon, and Jet *The Three Billy Goat's Gruff* and the *Berenstain Bears* and do different voices and read fast in some places, then slow down and make us beg for the next part." She smiled, like she could see a specific moment vividly.

"He played with his voice and stopped to add extra shit about the characters. Then, one day, he showed up at bedtime and ain't have no book. Moon asked him, 'You ain't gone read to us?'

"He said, 'Yeah! I got my own story.' We looked at his ass like his feet left the ground!" She got quiet for a second, then she said, "My brother could've wrote his own damn books." She eased her chin up and told me, "Could've been a teacher."

We held the rope in our hands, but hadn't started turning it, just stood there looking at Stacia, who wasn't a bad storyteller herself. She knew that we were waiting, that she had us. But this Stacia wasn't the one who showed up every day, ready to snap, using a volume of voice turned up too loud. She had seen things living in the same apartment as the gangsters running the world downstairs. This Stacia spoke softly.

"One day, Quan put the library books on the stove and burned them in front of all of us. Sweat watched the fire black out them words. 'You gone quit acting like a lil bitch,' Quan told him. Then he grabbed Sweat by the back of his neck and pushed him out the door.

"I went to the stove after they left, poked my fingers around the burnt pages, rubbed the black dust in my hands. It's crazy how quick something so special can turn to nothing."

Precious heard Stacia's words, but she was still missing a lot. She asked, "He read to you when he got home?"

Stacia stuck her neck out and called Precious stupid with her twisted-up face, but I cut in and told her, "They burned the books so that he could stop being soft." Then the look in her eyes told us that she'd gotten it. Stacia finished.

"Sweat ain't come home until the middle of the night. I waited and waited for him to show up with a story but dozed off. I jumped up when I heard his keys at the door. He turned on some music videos and lit a joint. When the smoke made it to my room, I went in there.

"First thing I notice is that Sweat got a black eye, busted lip, and he frowning. I sat next to him. We just stared at some girls popping all over the TV. I knew he got jumped in that day but he wasn't going to talk about it. I just asked, 'Where the story?' He shook his head from side to side. 'Tomorrow?' He did it again, this time, faster. I just went back to bed."

Her eyes got glossy, but she didn't cry. I could tell, even though she didn't say it, she cried herself to sleep that night. I knew too that she broke into this story so that I could prepare myself for the day that somebody burned Meechie's books.

EIGHT

Bombs Bursting in Air

We had time to change the mood before Tonya showed up that day, but I kept thinking about Stacia's story the whole time we played in the square.

When Tonya eventually arrived in some of the new clothes Mama gave her, smelling like the perfumed lotion, I told my friends that Mama said they were invited to join us for a trip downtown for the big fireworks event in Grant Park, which was held every year on July 3rd. So, for a while, they got all excited about going to see that, and I stopped thinking about Stacia's sad Sweat story.

Mama took me out of the neighborhood all the time, but Precious lived at her church, and both Stacia's and Tonya's lives seemed tethered to the block, so I knew a field trip was just what we all needed.

We had a few days to get ready for the trip, and we would all have colorful outfits and, thanks to Mama, freshly braided hair. We smiled at the thought of getting dressed up for an outing. You couldn't tell none of us that we weren't the cutest girls in the world.

On July 3rd, when the bus arrived, I wanted to sit next to Tonya. I let everybody go ahead of me. Stacia rushed on first and found a window seat, and Precious sat next to her. When Tonya got on, I let her have the window in our two-seater, and Mama sat behind us.

I enjoyed watching Tonya watch people out on the street. When the bus stopped to pick up more passengers, we all turned around to see who would get on. With thousands of people living on each block of South State Street, in those days, there was always something to see. We were easily amused, so if someone had to run to catch the bus, we'd crack up at their struggle.

On one block, people got wet up with Super Soakers; another corner just had people standing around, looking. A fire hydrant shot water high into the air, and we all leaned our faces into the window, wishing we could get off the bus and play. You only got a few minutes of this homemade waterpark before the firemen showed up, pissy.

At 48th Street, we were no longer amused. We saw a wrecking ball, and it sobered everyone's mood. "My building used to be right there," Stacia said, pointing to a wide-open space across from a building with wires hanging out the side.

"For real?" I asked her, because I didn't know what else to say.

Then Tonya looked at her with a sadness that said she understood exactly what Stacia felt. She stared out the window too, looking at the emptiness. But Stacia looked away. Reality snatched us out of our giggling moment. It was like that that summer: one minute we laughed loud and played hard, the next we were silent and worried.

The bus started moving again until we stopped at Beethoven. "That was my school," Stacia said, our depressed tour guide.

We all looked over at it, then Precious asked her, "You liked Beethoven better than Farren?"

Stacia thought about it for a minute, then said, "I never had friends like y'all when I was there."

Precious and I smiled at this; it was sweet to hear her talk about us like we were special. Tonya gave us a soft smile then turned back to the window. Precious returned to the novel she was reading. I watched my friends, and the people getting on and off the bus. Every once in a while, I'd catch Tonya looking at me, and we'd smile at each other.

As we drove, the buildings kept changing color every few blocks: red, then white, then red, then white, then red. Our version of the flag, these buildings, like crumbs we scraped up from the plate of somebody else's American Dream.

After 20th Street, when the projects ended, we crossed Roosevelt Road, and Tonya said, "This gotta be the biggest street in Chicago!" We got excited about that, then Precious snapped her head up from *The Coldest Winter Ever*, a novel Stacia took from one of her sisters that we'd been passing around our group.

She said, "King Drive is *wider*," then she found her spot in the book and kept reading.

"No, it's not!" I told her.

Then Stacia agreed with me, saying, "King Drive ain't bigger than this street!"

We started getting loud, so Mama stepped in. "Ladies?" We all looked at her. She said, "Inside voices."

Then I asked Mama, thinking she would settle it for us. "Which one is bigger?"

"I want *you* to find the answer," she said. We all groaned. It was a Ms. Pierce answer. Our teacher never told you the answer to questions *you* had. Once, somebody tried to settle this argument about Wacker Drive. They heard that it ran north and south, and somebody else said it went east and west. She sent us all home for the weekend to find the answer. Turns out, it was a trick question; in Chicago, Wacker Drive runs north, south, east, *and* west!

Right after our argument about Roosevelt Road, these boys in dingy white tees got on the bus, their ashy hands gripping scuffed-up mop buckets and drumsticks. As soon as they all sat down in the back of the bus, Stacia turned around, leaned past Mama, and yelled, "Y'all going to the fireworks?" Mama and the boys started talking at the same time, but Stacia heard her name, so she looked at Mama.

"Remember we talked about being a lady?"

Stacia just stared at her, like she couldn't remember. There was nothing about being a lady that got her excited. She probably tuned out that little speech right as it was coming out of Mama's mouth. She nodded anyway.

"Would a lady yell across an entire bus?"

"Sorry," she said, but then she snapped her head back, hoping the boys would repeat their answer.

At Balbo and State, we tumbled off the bus like clowns, in our red, white, and blue outfits. Me and Stacia jumped off the last step, our legs flying everywhere. Mama pulled us all aside right away and threatened to take us across the street to get back on the bus going home. We promised to act right. She made us hold hands, and we stomped down Balbo Street, up and over and down the bridge, and then Tonya spotted the Buckingham Fountain shooting water high into the sky.

"Look!" she said, louder than I ever heard her say anything.

Everybody said, "Oooh."

We walked and walked until we found a spot to put out the blankets. When we settled into a place on a hill, Mama let us roll around, while she snapped pictures of us enjoying the sky and lake and grass.

We played Uno and hand games and watched birds fight one another for scraps of food that people tossed on the ground. We were looking at the masses of white people, curious about who they were, and how they lived. I remembered what Quan told that kid he called Lil Man, that we had to move because white people wanted to be closer to their jobs.

His words would follow me around for years.

WHILE PRECIOUS AND STACIA WERE locked in a tense game of Uno, me and Tonya rolled down the hills a few more times. Out of earshot, Tonya said to me, "I wish we could stay here forever."

"We got enough food," I said.

"We could sleep right here in this grass!"

"And drink the water down there." I pointed at Lake Michigan, and Tonya wrinkled her nose. "We could fish, when we run out of sandwiches." She gave an audible sound of disgust after that, and we both laughed as we hiked back up the hill to where Mama had set up camp.

"I wish we ain't have to ever go back to the buildings," Tonya said, looking out toward the water. I enjoyed going to Grant Park too, but the serious look on her face reminded me about her life back at home, that her mama was probably doing drugs. I reached over and rubbed her back, and the motion seemed to bring tears to her eyes.

We were quiet for a second, then I heard Stacia yelling, "I beat her, Fe Fe! I finally won!"

———

IT GOT DARK, THEN REDS and golds started exploding in the sky. Tonya's mouth and eyes opened as wide as they could, as if she intended to catch all the colors, and Stacia looked so little and sweet for once, her face smooth, eyes soft and relaxed like they were preparing for tears to fall. Precious had the biggest smile on her face, and even though it was dark, and I couldn't prove it, I knew that red had spread all over her cheeks and forehead, because it happened every time she had a burst of joyful emotion.

Mama made some of the same *oohs* and *wows* right along with us. I enjoyed the fireworks, but I was irritated, even back then, by the patriotic music. It was too busy and loud and stiff. We had no context for that music, or why it always accompanied fireworks. We knew that it was for the Fourth of July, but when I was a kid, all that I knew was that no one had to work, and it seemed like the entire city of Chicago went downtown on July 3rd to watch the fireworks burst over the lake.

When only smoke covered the sky, we knew it was over. On the trip back across the bridge, we skipped together, swinging our arms and kicking rocks until we reached the fountain. The water shot straight up into the air as high as the second floor of our building, but also sprayed a misty sheet of water that floated across the area, like the open fire hydrant we saw hours before. This was much better; no one was coming to turn it off.

On the bus ride home, all my friends fell asleep, but Precious woke up, and like she'd just had a prophetic dream she said, "Come to church with me."

I'd known her my whole life, and this was the first time she'd invited me directly. She'd always told me about what she did in church and about her friends at church, but she hadn't come right

out and asked me to go with her. I'd find out later it was because she knew that Mama wouldn't let me. Mama heard her, and
looked from me to Precious, trying to see how I felt about it. I
didn't give either of them an answer, and instead, just nestled my
face in Mama's lap, and thought about those pretty colors bursting over the inky, blue lake.

Yes, there had been shooting all week. Yes, it was nighttime
when we got home, and yes, it wasn't safe to let those good feelings of our lakefront experience weaken our capacity to stay alert,
to move swiftly as we navigated crowds of gangsters and made
our way home, but what had just happened, this night of pleasure
and seeing my friends not only get along but really enjoy themselves, it mentally blocked out those reflexes to protect myself. So
when we descended the steps of the bus, I heard the shots, but I
wasn't the Fe Fe who was prepared for war; I was a kid, coming
home from a night of lights and giggles and euphoria. My reflexes were delayed, and though I could hear gunshots, I didn't
react right away. I was startled when Mama pushed us down into
the grassless dirt, away from the curb, whispering to stay there
while she tried to cover all of us with her body.

Precious started reciting the Shepherd's Psalm, low and ag-
gressive, and Mama joined in.

> *Yea, though I walk through the valley of the shadow of death,*
> *I will fear no evil: for thou art with me;*
> *thy rod and thy staff they comfort me.*

I didn't know it yet, so I just listened to the words. I kept
thinking about other things though, worried that someone would

run up on us, and shoot us at close range while we huddled on the ground. Down there in the dirt, I wondered about two things: Meechie; was he in the window, this time looking for us? And when did Mama learn that Bible verse?

We stayed down there so long that my hand started tingling, falling asleep.

WHEN SHE THOUGHT IT WAS safe, Mama said, "When I say go, we're going to run as fast as we can into the building. Up to my apartment. I'm right here, so don't look back. Just run. Do you understand?" We said, "Yeah," and "Yes," and Mama said, "Come on!" but when I rose and jumped forward, only three of us—me, Precious, and Mama—ran. I looked back and saw Stacia on the ground holding her ankle and Tonya curled tight in a ball, like a snail. Me and Mama headed back for them, but Precious never stopped, running full speed for the building like Mama told her. She looked so free, running in that open field. And it should've been a normal sight, a child running through a playground, but in that moment, it was the most dangerous thing she could've done.

Tonya wasn't moving and lay so completely still that she looked unconscious. I crouched down and leaned close to her, trying to see if she'd flinch or if there was any rise in her body. Mama scooped Stacia up off the ground. Stacia hollered and reached for her left ankle. When Mama called Tonya's name, trying to get her to uncurl herself, there was no answer. She called her again. Nothing. When she gently turned her, there was a flinch at Mama's touch.

"Tonya, baby, can you look at me?" Tonya shook her head no, still curled tight in a ball. I was relieved that she was still breathing. Mama put Stacia down, and said, "Fee, help her walk."

Then she went over and lifted Tonya up, and we walked as fast as we could toward the building. It was quiet then, like we were the only four people in the world.

Back home, we crouched down in the hallway, and Mama called out for Meechie, who, after a while, opened his bedroom door and answered her. He wasn't wearing a shirt. He walked to the hallway and sat down. He looked concerned for Stacia, who was moaning from her injuries; she had sprained her ankle, and it had already begun to swell, looking puffier than her other skinny one. Me and Mama weren't physically hurt, but when we heard banging on the door, the trauma of the night they took Meechie rose up in my throat, all sour and hot.

Mama arched forward, attempting to get up, and Meechie pushed her onto the floor. Her shoulder connected with the wall. We all looked at him like he was crazy. Mama, all confused, tried to get up again.

With his hand still holding her shoulder, he softened his look, and said, "Last time, they choked me until I couldn't breathe." Mama reached for him, hugging him, and he looked at me with these helpless eyes that I'd never seen.

The banging continued, and every time they hit the door, Mama jumped and Tonya seemed to sink deeper into her knees. Stacia watched us, her face crunched up from pain. She said to Mama, almost under her breath, "They won't come in unless you open the door." This didn't calm Mama down; she just held her boy, who was a sophomore at DuSable, but who had by then already left boyhood behind.

Again, I tucked my face into Mama's stomach. Eventually the banging stopped, and we knew that the police had passed over our door.

NINE

Project Kids

The next day, on July 4th, Mama summoned Auntie Nora's husband, Uncle Tim, to come and take us to their house for a week until things cooled down on the block. Auntie Nora was Mama's little sister by four years, and that summer, she was thirty.

Uncle Tim looks like a cop. It's the stiffness where his neck and shoulder merge, and how he keeps this serious face, even if he's just cracked a joke. He'll give you eye contact, but don't expect his brows to move too much. His lips stay smashed into one thick line. Hands always clenched, as if pondering injustice. He walks with both pounce and sway because he's swole.

You see him, and think he's been in jail or the army or in somebody's gang, but he hasn't. You would never guess that he actually does math all day; he's an accountant at a firm in the Loop. Underneath those starched shirts he wears to work, there's a horseshoe branded in his skin from his HBCU days. Every time he drove over to the buildings to get us, the dudes in the parking lot panicked, assuming he was a plainclothes, coming to lock them up.

They'd yell the signal for everyone to scatter, then one of the older leaders would say, "Dude straight," and things would instantly calm down.

Uncle Tim always came up to our apartment, talked to Mama for a little while, then reached for my weekend bag, carrying it all the way to the car. That day, he held my hand as we walked through the breezeway and made Meechie walk in front of him, as if he got paid to protect us. We climbed into his mountain of a truck, and I crawled to the very last row of seats because I liked it back there, by myself. Meechie sat in the passenger seat, and once Uncle Tim got in, he said, "Seat belts," then his truck crunched over glass and pop cans and rolled onto State Street.

At the corner, where my school sat on the left, the truck turned right onto 51st Street. We all looked over at the police station as we drove toward the highway entrance, remembering our incident there. Uncle Tim drove by the white buildings, then the red ones in the Hole, and after that, we'd put miles between us and the Robert Taylor Homes, going up the Dan Ryan to the hundreds.

With the music on, and two rows of seats in front of me, I couldn't hear what Meechie and Uncle Tim were saying, but they looked nice together. For a while, on these rides to Auntie Nora's, I pretended that Uncle Tim was my bodyguard and driver, and I bet Meechie fantasized that he had a dad. Mama wouldn't talk much about our real father; we just knew that he was absent. That he decided to leave one day and didn't come back. It was the story of just about everyone we knew, except Precious.

Though they weren't related by blood, it was easy to mistake Meechie and Uncle Tim as father and son. They had a matching deep brown skin color, similar mannerisms, and neither one of them were ever in a hurry to talk. They both listened to gangster rap, so Uncle Tim played a Bone Thugs-N-Harmony CD. At first,

I thought he was trying to look cool for Meechie, his nephew from the *'jets*—as they used to call the projects back when he was younger in the '70s—but later on, I'd learn that Uncle Tim got into rap when he was a boy living on the South Side.

Watching Meechie up there laughing and telling a story made me relax. I thought maybe that horrible experience of going to jail was something that he had put behind him—which was naive of me. He looked so happy sitting in that passenger seat. I was in my own world in the back, hoping that Uncle Tim could teach him about manhood and how to live on our crazy block.

While Meechie and Uncle Tim caught up, I played That's My Car, which is exactly what it sounds like, and the ride took long enough for me to collect a million cars on the Dan Ryan Expressway, past the McDonald's on 69th, the Toys"R"Us on 87th, and the big Greyhound buses on 95th Street.

THEIR HOUSE ON LASALLE STREET was such a pretty place, painted blue and white or gray and white, depending on how the sun hit it. The houses on their block weren't cookie-cut. One was yellow and white, another had a red trim. Even the name of the neighborhood sounded nice: *Roseland*. Since traffic only went one way, we played in the streets, which I wasn't ever able to do on State Street, a wide, busy street that took people all the way downtown.

My aunt's house had a swing on the porch and flowers and pretty rocks on each side of the steps, and the grass was a green that would hurt your eyes if you stared at it too long.

No one on the block stepped on other people's grass. In my neighborhood, there wasn't any grass to protect. We had a bunch of dirt, no trees, and trash tornadoes spinning around on windy days. It was everyone's and no one's building, so we couldn't love it like you'd care for a house of your own. Kids punished it with markers and spray paint. They peed on the stairs. They tossed Cheeto bags on the ground and spit sunflower seeds on the elevator floor. But even though Auntie Nora's house was nice, it faced other houses on a tiny street. When I looked out my window, I saw the sky and clouds and sun. It was the only thing we had going for us in the projects; the view was amazing.

Three trains went by my building: in the distance, the Red Line El, the Metra, and a freight train that moved incredibly slow, and made the most noise, carrying huge boxes. Outside of the window everything was moving away. Maybe it was a warning that things rarely stayed the same.

As soon as I climbed out of the car, Auntie Nora leaped from the porch swing and clamped me into a tight hug with her bony arms, calling me "Fish!" and filling my hands with fake jewelry she'd ordered from Avon catalogs. I was the girl she tried to have, while Meechie was the boy that Uncle Tim used to be: curious, strong, and misunderstood. They had one thirteen-year-old son, my cousin Tim Junior, who we called TJ. The only thing he had in common with me and Meechie was our genetics.

We split up into teams of girls and boys, so me and Auntie Nora jumped into her red Altima and zipped over to Evergreen Plaza, this huge mall that was only a few minutes away.

Auntie Nora always had questions about Mama, but I had been warned about talking too much. Even though Mama and Auntie Nora were sisters, they still kept secrets, something I didn't understand at the time. I thought if I had a sister, I'd tell her everything.

She wanted to know about the buildings, and that's when I remembered that she used to live in 4950 too, that once, she and

Mama were like me and Meechie: just kids running up and down the porches and buying candy from someone like Ms. Rose.

We walked around the mall, and even though it wasn't my birthday, Auntie Nora got me three new outfits, a pair of jelly sandals, and some lip gloss. She bought me whatever snacks I wanted, and by the time I'd stuffed myself with pizza slices and pretzels, and started in on an ice-cream cone, I realized I'd been talking too much.

"Your mama tell you where she want to move to?"

"She won't tell me nothing," I said, rolling my eyes. She laughed.

"I told her she ought to move on out here. Then I could see you all the time!"

I thought about what it might feel like to live in Roseland, where maybe I wouldn't have to drop to the ground to evade bullets. "Were you scared to leave the projects?"

"No, I couldn't wait to get out and see something different! I got married in the middle of college, real young, and it seems like I've lived away from the projects longer than I lived in them." She paused for a second, then said, "That's how it's going to be with you. I can tell you've got people to see, things to do!" I smiled at the thought of being that way, like her. Mama's things to do were always for me and my brother. Auntie Nora seemed to live a life of adventure and freedom. Even though she had a son, she somehow managed to go off and do what she wanted without him.

Mama and Auntie Nora were really different. There were obviously things you'd notice right away, like Auntie Nora's desire to dive into things enthusiastically, but if you were paying closer attention, you'd see their values in how they raised their kids. Mama worked hard to make sure that me and Meechie were respectful of people and the things in our home, even though we lived around some wild people and we didn't have many things in our home worth much value. Auntie Nora and Uncle Tim seemed to let TJ have whatever he wanted and go anywhere. I'd later learn that they trusted him, and that he *was* aware of the dangers in Roseland.

AFTER OUR SHOPPING SPREE, WE headed back to the house on La-Salle. Uncle Tim and the boys were not hanging at all. What really happened that day was that Uncle Tim slipped into the basement, and the boys did whatever they wanted, separately. TJ and his friends huddled around a PlayStation even though he was supposed to be with Meechie, who wasn't anywhere in sight.

I wandered around the house deep in thought until I heard a familiar sound coming from outside: the *tick-tick-tick-tick* of a double Dutch game. I ran to the window and saw a handful of girls jumping. They were new to the block. I had one friend who lived directly across the street, but she was visiting family someplace else for the summer.

I watched the unfamiliar girls jump, missing my friends back home. One of them saw me in the window, staring, and she waved me over. "You wanna play?" she called. I nodded.

"You can get Erica's end," she said. I turned, and they jumped, and we played for a while. Everything was cool until somebody asked, "Don't you live in the projects?" Before I could answer, another voice said, "The projects?" Then she looked me up and down and said, "But you so clean." And just like that, I was mad and ready to fight.

"I'm supposed to be dirty?" I said, a hand on my hip, neck stuck all out, mouth open, channeling Stacia.

The girl had a list and tried to count out several insults, poking out fingers from a curled fist while saying, "I bet you on public aid, you don't know your daddy—" I looked past the girl at the neat colorful homes that lined LaSalle Street. Those people lived in houses owned by their families. I lived in the projects, where no one owned anything, where we paid our rent with government checks that came in the mail on the first of the month.

I didn't hear what else she had to say. I just asked her, "You want your ass whupped?" because that's what Stacia would say.

"What?" she asked, getting in my face. I pushed her. Then when she ran up on me again, I pushed her so hard that she hit the ground. Before she could get up, somebody stole off me, right in the jaw, and I stumbled backward. It looked like the houses on the block were moving, but really, I was falling. The girl who called me dirty was cursing me out, and someone kept kicking me in the side. I felt something wet hit me and was pretty sure it was spit. My cousin and his friends appeared and tried to break up the fight, and everybody from porches and the baseball game down the street came over to see the action.

Other people jumped in the fight, and in the confusion, I got to limp away. Before I made it to Auntie Nora's porch, I heard someone say, "Cause she from the projects." That hurt more than those kicks to my side. I wanted to go home. Even though there were bullets popping all over the place and police constantly banging at our door.

When Auntie Nora saw me, with my jaw and lip all puffed up, clothes dirty and disheveled, and scratches on my arms from the concrete, she leaped up from her sofa and squealed, "Fish! Baby, who did this to you?" The concern and care melted my hard facade, and the tears gushed. I couldn't get the answer out. She scowled at her son and asked him the question.

"These girls she was jumping rope with," he said, hunching his shoulders.

While Auntie Nora patched me up, Meechie stumbled through the door, his friend holding him up; he was in worse shape. I thought my aunt was going to faint. "Oh my God! Tim!" Her voice seemed to fill the entire house then, and Uncle Tim appeared, ready to fight.

He saw me and Meechie, and then he understood the panic in her voice.

I had skinned knees and my side hurt, but my brother's right eye was swollen shut, his nose slanted a little bit, and he was hold-ing his side. What bothered me the most, though? His Raiders cap was on his head, twisted to the right. It seemed like a hat would be the first thing you'd lose if you got jumped. Auntie Nora drove us to the hospital, and Uncle Tim rushed back to the building to get Mama.

Once we were all at the hospital together, Mama went to Meechie's room, and I stayed back in the waiting room with my aunt, uncle, and cousin.

"Why weren't you two together?" Auntie Nora asked her son.

"He didn't want to play the game with us," he told her. And it was true, Meechie wasn't really into video games.

"Why didn't you stay with him?" Auntie Nora asked. TJ looked at his shoes.

Uncle Tim rescued him, and said, "Meechie was probably on Perry with Manny."

TJ didn't say anything, just stared back at them, not giving Meechie up. I didn't know what Perry Street or Manny meant, but it seemed to answer something for them all.

"Did they jump Manny?" Auntie Nora asked.

"No," Uncle Tim said.

TJ's face wanted to say so much, but even though he and Meechie weren't tight, no one wanted to be called a snitch. Mama appeared in the waiting room and told us that we could come see him. Meechie sat up on a thin bed, his chest bandaged, nose wrapped, an eye still closed and purple. We just looked at him, like a creature we didn't know. Only Mama and Auntie Nora dared to touch him and throw sympathetic looks his way.

Uncle Tim and TJ kept some distance, just nodding at him, barely laughing at Auntie Nora's jokes about how he looked like a mummy. When she said Meechie could stay at her house and heal there over the summer, believing it was an isolated incident, that her house was still safer than our building, Uncle Tim cut in and said, "No. He needs to go home."

We all snapped our heads in his direction, but he was still looking at Meechie. When Auntie Nora said, "Timothy!" he only moved his eyes in her direction. Before she could assert herself, Uncle Tim seemed to communicate something with his clenched jaw and the stern expression on his face. She looked over at her sister with an apology, and Mama said, "I'll take him home."

Just like that, Uncle Tim had cast Meechie out, and we'd taken sides; every household squaring up, Auntie Nora not sure what her husband knew but trusting his decision. The quiet tension in the room made the beeping machines and TV show playing over our heads seem way too loud. *He needs to go home*, that's what Uncle Tim said. I needed to go home too.

TEN

Name-Calling

I went home wounded, hating my uncle for ejecting my brother from his house. I kept thinking about the looks Uncle Tim and TJ had on their faces. Initially, I wondered, *Do they know something that we don't?* but then resolved that they too had labeled us project kids. The truth was that I spent all my time around project kids, and when I discovered what kind of things they got into, I didn't like some of it, but they were my friends, and I wasn't going to stop playing with them. That girl in Roseland had called me a project kid, and it was the one slur I couldn't get out of my head that whole summer.

At a pretty early age, I learned that people used names to tear one another down, so I'd become sensitive to name-calling. Later in college, I'd study history and discover that one of the first acts of a colonizer is to take away a captured person's name and give them a new one.

When we're young, this is especially true because we're already ashamed about our teeth or the shape of our heads or how our ears stick out or about our hair length, underdeveloped bod-

ies, overdeveloped bodies, family history, sexual activities, or lack
of sexual activities. Anything can make you vulnerable to name-
calling, and those names cut into the skin sometimes, enter the
bloodstream. Somehow that summer, I stumbled upon an important fact about naming: it also has the power to build people up.

When I start to date in college, my collection of intimate pet
names will run the gamut of well-thought-out, uplifting names,
like Stevie—a play on my last name, Stevens. Fe Fe will stick
around. Baby will return, it's my go-to, for some reason, and works
only when I'm in a truly intimate relationship with a man. But
something else will happen as I age. I will return to Felicia, and it
will feel like a prestigious name.

For a while it will hold, and then, it will seem to dissipate al-
together when I step into dual roles of teacher at an academy and
youth pastor of a church. Then, I'll become Pastor Stevie. Before
the community settles on this title for me, when I'm still little
Fe Fe from Robert Taylor, I will ingest too many disgusting,
spirit-breaking insults floating in the atmosphere, some meant
for me, others, like stray bullets, piercing tissue because I happened to be standing nearby while the violence ensues.

AFTER RETURNING HOME FROM ROSELAND, feeling awful, I didn't
have the nerve to go to Tonya's house and deal with her dragon
of a mother. I went to get Precious instead, and just hoped
Tonya would come by. I saw Stacia down in the playground sitting on the bench's back, her feet on the seat: *Project kid behavior,*
I thought. I called her name through the gate, something I didn't
usually do, and she ran into the building and all the way upstairs.
Even though she smelled like a skunk, from sitting around people smoking weed, I was so glad to see her. She joined us in the

square, and we started a game. I watched the stairs every chance I got, but Tonya didn't come down that evening. Though I didn't have everyone, it felt good to be back home with my friends, who in that moment felt like family.

I DIDN'T KNOW WHY, BUT the next day at school, Stacia had an attitude.

Precious could feel it too; she kept looking at us look at each other. Stacia sat at the front of the class, next to Ms. Pierce, while me and Precious got sandwiched between the masses of students. We sat kitty-corner to one another, though, so we smirked and winked at each other all day.

Stacia wanted to talk about Tonya. She must've seen her do something on the block while I was away, and I guess she'd been thinking about it the whole time I was at my aunt's house. She couldn't wait to get me alone. When we had our first group bathroom trip, she stood outside my stall until I swung it open.

"How come you brought that dirty girl in the square?"

I pushed past her and went to wash my hands at the sink, concentrating hard on the spaces between fingers, washing like they were caked in dried paint.

"You know she nasty, right?"

I kissed my teeth, thinking Stacia was making up lies. I grabbed some paper towels, but she snatched them out of my hand.

"I'm so serious, Fee! People gone think we like that too! You don't know nothing about that girl."

"I ain't know nothing about you neither," I told her, in a much smaller voice. Ms. Pierce would burst in any minute because Stacia's voice was on boom. She looked hurt, and before she could recover, I rushed out of the bathroom.

It wasn't entirely true; I knew a lot about Stacia before I asked her to play rope. I knew that she came from a family of gangsters, and people all over the school—every grade—were afraid to have a Buchanan in their class. But I reached out anyway, knowing good and well that she could turn on me, any day, like some pet that was cuddly and a great companion, then up and bit you just because.

She wouldn't let it go, so at lunch, I told her part of the truth. "She needed some friends."

"Ain't have to be us," she said, still looking at me with her head tilted and mouth open, the way she did when she wanted to keep an argument going. I just ate my lunch and talked to Precious, who couldn't stay calm and had blushed all red because of our heated discussion. So I looked at Stacia and told her, "I want to be her friend. You ain't got to be."

She made a face that said *I know*, and we left it at that.

That should've been a clue.

Maybe I could've worked harder that day to change her mind about Tonya. Or maybe I should've done what she said, told Tonya that she couldn't play with us anymore. Maybe I could've done something, anything different. But I liked Tonya's sweet spirit and thought things would eventually work out for our little friend group. Stacia huffed and puffed and screwed up her face the entire lunch period, but she still showed up to play rope that afternoon, so I thought we were good and she'd gotten over it.

TONYA FOUND US JUST BEFORE the streetlights blinked on. Since I'd first invited her a few weeks prior, she'd come to the square almost every day, but you just never knew what time. It was as if she had a full-time job and adult responsibilities to handle before she could come and play with us. I remember exactly when things changed, and I barely saw her anymore; it was the day that these dudes came and grabbed her.

We played a few rounds, then we heard the sound of fast feet on the stairs. We got excited because we thought it was Ricky and Derrick. Stacia swiped some thick, shiny lip gloss on her lips, and I had my hand in my hair before I realized what I was doing, but it wasn't Ricky, Derrick, and Jon Jon. It was a group of dudes from downstairs. I didn't know their names, but they were definitely not boys, and I knew that they were gangsters by all the jewelry draped around their necks and the white tees they were wearing. The one who seemed to be in charge did all the talking. He looked right at Tonya and said, "Come on." Tonya dropped the rope, didn't even say bye to us, and followed him.

"See you tomorrow, Tonya," I said.

Stacia rolled her eyes at me.

Tonya stopped walking and turned back to say something to me, but the guy yanked her shirt by the neckline, literally dragging her away while telling us, "Shawty gotta go."

They all went down the stairs. When he called her Shawty, on a day when I was so sensitive to name-calling, I knew right away that she wasn't safe. Like she heard me thinking, Stacia said, "She a hoe." The words came out sharp and quick, and stung like a paper cut. It even shocked Precious, whose eyes popped wide at the accusation.

"She ain't no hoe!" I hollered, and it was loud because it wasn't five seconds before Mama opened our screen door and called me.

"She is! Look at all these dudes in her face. You think they wanna play *rope* with her?"

Mama hung out the door, and I was pretty sure I was in trouble because I couldn't even say *lie* in my house. A real curse word would mean instant punishment: days stuck in the house and no

TV. "Felicia?" Mama called, and because I wasn't even Fe Fe, I knew that she heard the cursing.

"Yes, Mama?" I said, walking down the porch in a hurry.

"Come here!"

I ran to the door, getting my story together in the short distance.

"You out here cursing?"

"No, Mama! That was Stacia," I told her. She actually believed me, knowing how wild Stacia could be, but she still wanted me to come in the house.

She said, "Go get your rope."

I went back to the square and snatched the strings off the ground, not even saying, "I gotta go," or "See you tomorrow." I just rolled my eyes at Stacia.

She whispered, "She still a hoe." I kept walking like I didn't hear it, but her words hit my ears heavy and got into my head. *Hoe: a girl who'll have sex with anybody, no matter their age or status, no matter where: incinerator, stairway, car, elevator.* I didn't want to believe Tonya was a hoe, so I dismissed it as a reflex insult, resolving that Stacia was just mad that our game had to end and that Tonya was getting so much attention from guys, but there was much more going on than my innocent mind could imagine.

THE NEXT DAY, I WOKE up before the sun, still thinking about what Stacia called Tonya. I didn't have anywhere to go so early, but I was wide awake. I got out of bed and went to the kitchen for some cereal, walking slow and soft so I didn't wake up Mama. On the way to the kitchen, I saw out of the living room window a little bit of the prettiest orange rising over the back of DuSable.

It was sunshine, trying to bust through the curtain of clouds like a diva.

I stood there, my forehead stuck to the child-safety bars, staring at it. The playground was empty. I looked over at Tonya's old building and wondered if that's where she met those dudes from yesterday. The life had been sucked out of her high-rise, one family at a time, but there was the sun, shining down on what was left of it. The pink and orange colors spread out all over the sky, shining beauty on our block. I sat in the window for a while, enjoying the show. Then I saw Mama Pearl walk out of the building with her purse strapped across her body. She kept her head up, moving quickly for a little old lady, then got into her Buick and sped off.

I got my cereal, sat on the couch, and turned on the TV. I ended up falling asleep there, and when I woke up, I was covered with a blanket, and the cereal bowl was gone. Mama had come through, probably watched me sleep, wondered when and why I had migrated into the living room. Most people don't think about their relationships with their mothers until they have children of their own, and want to take the good things from their parenting skills, but too many kids on my block had moms who were into some strange and dangerous things. That summer, I kept tilting my head to the side, looking at Mama with warmth in my eyes, knowing already that I was fortunate to have her.

By two o'clock, I was still home, sitting on the floor doing a puzzle. Mama stuck her head in my room and gave me a look because I hadn't even tried to go outside. Stacia called Tonya a hoe, and she knew it would hurt me. One of us had to fix things, but that day, I decided it wouldn't be me.

"Fee," Mama called, and I was glad to be back to Fee, but I didn't want to talk.

"Yes, Mama?"

"You feeling okay?"

"Yes, Mama."

"So why aren't you outside? It's a nice day, and you're staying in?"

I started picking at a scab; it had been a day since those girls jumped me, and already a wound on my knee was trying to heal.

"Stop that!" Mama said, before asking, "Is it because you and Stacia had an argument?"

I just looked at her.

"You're moping around the house and playing by yourself as if you don't have a friend in the world. *Something* is going on."

I blurted out, "Mama, Stacia get on my nerves."

"What about Precious and Tonya?" she said with her eyes all happy like she'd helped me figure things out. For some reason, I didn't tell her about those boys. I couldn't tell her that some gangbangers came and took Tonya off the porch. I couldn't tell her that Stacia accused her of being a hoe. I couldn't tell her that stuff. I couldn't, but I knew that if I didn't tell her something, she wouldn't leave me alone.

"I could play with them," I finally said, trying to act like she gave me a brand-new idea.

I got dressed and went straight to the tenth floor to get Tonya. I pushed my shoulders back, raised my chin, and got ready to meet Rochelle, this woman who was always in a snotty mood.

I needed to know that Tonya was okay. I didn't even knock twice before the door opened like somebody was expecting me. Rochelle said, "What?" and it was nasty, like I knocked on her door every hour with stupid questions.

My eyes and words stuttered at first, then I pulled it together and asked, "Can Tonya come out?"

"She ain't here," she said, and slammed the door in my face. I stood there, my eyes tearing up because she hurt my feelings. I felt stupid and disrespected, and then I started to get scared for

Tonya. Was Tonya, a twelve-year-old, still out with those three older dudes since last night? I ran down the stairs and jumped over the last three, but my heart wasn't in it. On the eighth floor, I walked over to the elevator and waited. I heard voices on the floor below me, familiar voices, so I squinted my eyes and leaned my head closer to the stairs. I couldn't make out words, but one voice sounded like my brother's.

Meechie had a broken nose and ribs, and an eye that was trying its best to open up. There was no way he was outside, and doing what? I tiptoed down to the seventh floor. It looked like my brother, but this boy was wearing a white tee, with jeans I didn't recognize, Tommy boxers I hadn't ever seen, and Timberland boots Meechie didn't own. He stood with half his body in the garbage room, half out.

When I heard him say, "I'll be back," I felt the sensation of fingers running down the back of my neck. It *was* my brother. He reached his arm up and made a sound because he was still in pain. His fingers locked and twisted with this other dude's, then froze in the air to make a gang sign.

"Aight, Folks," the other guy said to him. Then he smirked and turned in my direction. He called my brother *Folks*.

As Meechie approached me, I opened my mouth a few times to say something, but nothing came out. Then he saw me, and before I could talk, he clamped his hand under my armpit and pulled me toward the stairs, wincing from the pain of his injuries.

"What you doing up here?" he asked.

"What *you* doing up here?" I tried to deliver the words with attitude, but I had to keep myself from falling as he dragged me down the stairs.

"Don't worry about me. Get yo' ass out of this stairway."

I started crying. I don't know if it was because of the way

he was talking to me or because he was a gangbanger or because he was hurting me. I couldn't even see the stairs after a while, because the tears rushed down my face so fast. My feet seemed to melt, and I fell. Meechie looked down at me. He tried to stay tough, screaming, "Get up!" I tried, but I didn't have control over my body anymore. He looked down at me, weeping all over the ground, and then he said, "Fee, come on, man." He squatted down and tried to pull me up. I sat up, real slow.

"You got jumped in at Auntie Nora's house? That's what you was doing on Perry!" I screamed at him. He just looked at his Tims.

"You gone tell Mama?" he asked. He helped me up. I wiped my face and just looked at him, my brother, a newly initiated gang-ster. I hunched my shoulders, because I didn't know if I should tell or not.

His secret wouldn't last much longer than it took for his face to heal. I came in for water one afternoon and saw Mama sitting at the kitchen table with that saggy look that she had at the police precinct. There was a black pistol and a few tiny bags of crystal nuggets on the table where we eat. "Go to your room," Mama said with no energy. I knew it was Meechie's, that he was caught.

From my room, I heard the front door open, and Meechie said, "Ma."

She said, "Ma my ass! You got this shit in my house?"

"Man—"

"I am *not* a man," she hollered.

"I know," he said, a smirk in his voice. Then her chair screeched back from the table, and I heard the clap of her palm hitting his skin.

"Hit me again," he said. "Do it. Everybody else do. Just punch on Meechie, he deserve it, right? This shit ends today," he shouted. "Tired of people putting they hands on me."

I heard him coming down the hall, those boots stomping hard. He passed my door and went to his room. Mama's voice echoed down the hallway as she followed him. When she said, "Not in my house! You will not disrespect me and live here," her sentence clipped off at the end.

It was too quiet, so I eased out of my room, and that's when I saw Meechie pull a long shotgun out of the inside of his dresser. I stood in the doorway of my room and watched him grab more guns: two more from the rip in his mattress. Like a magician, he summoned them, then made them disappear into a duffel bag.

He stomped out of his room. Mama screamed at the back of his head, "Don't try to come back!"

He didn't respond to this, but when he got to my door, he slowed down and looked at me. "You told her, huh?"

That's the last thing he said to me, that accusation, before he left.

MAMA WENT TO HER ROOM and closed the door. Meechie slammed the front door. I stood there in that empty hallway, not because bullets were flying outside, but because it's where we always went to be safe. I slid down the wall and sat on the floor. In the distance, on State Street, somebody's truck was playing *Down for My Niggaz*, the same song that Meechie rapped the night that he came home from the police station. My brother had walked out on us, had left us for the streets. That day, me and Mama got new names too: *them other niggas*.

ELEVEN

Cowboy Camp

I remember, the morning after he left, going into Meechie's room, taking deep breaths in there, inhaling the scents that he'd left behind: A vile, sour odor clinging to socks lying in the corner. The lingering scent of Cool Water cologne, still heavy on the pillowcase. I sat on his bed, still a mess. He was gone, but bits of him clung to those cotton fibers. He'd left dishes on his dresser. Drawers still wide-open, exposing T-shirts that I'd start wearing. One knock-off Nike lay on its side in the closet, a pair he hadn't worn in years. His room was a museum of a boy who once was. A boy who'd never come back.

I wrote in my journal a lot more after Meechie walked out. I'd stashed a photo of us in the back, between blank pages. We were just kids, four and eight in the snapshot. By the time I got to those sheets, and saw his sweet smile again, I'd begun writing about the unimaginable things that happened that summer.

Mama attacked Meechie's room that first afternoon after he left, cleaning it with bleach. She erased his essence. I started going in his room more often, just to look out the window. He had a view of the fire lane, a road running between State and Federal Streets, where there was more foot traffic than fire trucks. We lived sandwiched between State and Federal, the government on both sides of us at all times.

The thing was, I couldn't figure out whose fault it was. Why we lost him to the streets. I kept trying to blame someone. I accused everybody. I started with Grandma. She had him watching *Gunsmoke* and those Clint Eastwood Westerns when he was a little boy. I was too little to remember this, but he'd told me that he'd watch black-and-white dusty Westerns with her when she was alive. I thought maybe that's where it all started. Mama was guilty too; she let him see those Chuck Norris and Jean-Claude Van Damme movies and, every week, kung fu films on Samurai Sundays. Did this make him think about fighting all the time? Did he want to be tough like those actors? He listened to West Coast classics too, and got a rush every time he heard Eazy-E say, *Motherfuck Dre, motherfuck Snoop, motherfuck Death Row.*

He soaked up the conflict, let it rush through his veins. I could point my finger at so many people, but now I know better. My brother has always been different from me. When he heard gunshots, he stuck his face against the window. Most people got scared, but that *wop, wop, wop* of bullets hyped him up.

That summer, the war outside our window gave him a lot to see: our red building constantly going at it with the white buildings on the Low End. It all excited him: the guns, how the dudes in the playground stood like men, shoulders back, face stern, puffing on a cigarette or weed. They were cowboys, and our block, a cowboy camp.

I remember when we were kids, Meechie used to crash his trucks into the wall or other trucks, making so much noise. Then he started having all these guns. First, the neon-colored ones that squirted water. Next he got a Nerf gun with these foam balls. When plastic wasn't gangster enough, he got a BB gun. It was steel and looked like a real pistol. He didn't shoot people with it, but he hit things in the house, cereal boxes or my stuffed animals, working on his aim when Mama was asleep. Later, he told me that even before he moved out, even before he left, he never went out without a gun.

"You just feel naked," he said.

And didn't every cowboy carry? Loaded and unlocked, just in case he had to duel? Wasn't it part of the uniform? Hat, not the silly kind, curled on both ends, but a baseball cap, banged to the side. Vest: bulletproof. Boots: Tims, of course. Saggy jeans, gun hidden under his shirt. I tried to figure out when my brother turned into a cowboy, but then it hit me: maybe he'd always been one. Was it the day he came home from Michael Reese hospital, wrapped in that thin white blanket, teal stripe across the bottom, little cloth cap on his head? He was nursed by Mama, rocked and fed, but only until he was of age.

Stacia's words came back to me then: "He at that age, Fe Fe." And this was the reason for her story about Sweat. She tried to tell me that they'd eventually snatch him from us and introduce him to his new family.

It didn't matter if Mama nurtured or ignored him; the cowboys watched, waited for him, and then they decided it was time. He didn't go far. I watched my brother, the new cowboy, in action right outside our window.

The worst part about Cowboy Camp is that the person who no longer belongs to you runs and jumps and shoots right where you can see. I wonder if that would've made it easier, if we didn't have to watch Meechie downstairs, see him in his new skin. Most days, I'd see him lounging in the playground or standing guard at the building's entrance. While Stacia talked to her brothers and everybody knew that she was a Buchanan, Meechie tried not to interact with me when he was with the other guys, but if I caught him alone, we'd exchange a few words.

Me and Mama handled Meechie's absence differently; I snooped around, trying to keep him close, whatever was left of him in the house, but Mama wouldn't come out of her room until she had to go to the bathroom. I didn't have the word *depression* back then, but I remember thinking that Mama had dipped into a heavy sadness. His absence slowed her down and made her sleep all the time. I'd take advantage of her weakened state and wander around the building by myself, and sometimes when it was dark, which was against Mama's rules. In fact, no adult in my life would've advised this.

I HADN'T SEEN TONYA SINCE those guys dragged her out of the square a few days before, and I missed her. I figured she had to be home, that maybe she was on punishment or something. I went back to the ten.

Little kids buzzed around her porch, a loud, singing swarm. Four girls squared up playing Rockin' Robin, two kids skated up and down the porch in these blue-and-yellow skates that never glided like skates were supposed to. Both kids pushed, their faces concentrating hard, because they had a skate on one foot, a gym shoe on the other. Some kids stood around eating candy and talking, and three little boys rode around on bikes.

They blocked my way, so as I walked up, the girls broke up their square, right in the middle of "tweet, tweet, tweet." One of them said, "Ain't yo' name Fe Fe?" She was a tall, skinny girl, with her hair pointing every which way, even though it was ten o'clock in the morning. I knew right away that she was the Stacia of this group.

I smiled, and said, "Yeah."

"You play with Tonya."

I nodded.

"She ain't never in the house," the girl told me. But I kept walking. If she wasn't there, I planned to tell her mama about the boys. I knocked on the door, soft at first. No one answered. I knocked again, with tight knuckles, nervous about what I was about to say. I heard somebody yelling on the other side, and as they got closer, I could make out the words. The woman was saying, "Alright! Alright! Damn!" Then the door yanked open, and Tonya's mama, all upset, looked me up and down, and said, "She still ain't here."

"She got a boyfriend?" I asked.

She laughed, then said, "Shit, she got *boyfriends*." Then the door was closing.

I stuck my foot in before it closed, and asked, "You know where she at?"

"Lil girl, if you don't move that foot, and get away from this here door," she said, closing her eyes, emphasizing an unspoken threat.

"These boys took her!" I said.

She laughed again. "Ain't nobody *took* her."

The little kids watched us, their hand games not as interesting anymore. Then, like she a whole different person, she got quiet, her face stopped twisting into ugly, and she asked, "Baby, you got a couple dollars?" I shook my head from side to side and frowned a little. I didn't know why she wasn't taking this seriously.

"You ain't got no money?" she asked, tilting her head to the side, her face going back to scary. I moved my head faster, hoping it would convince her. I had a dollar and thirty cents, but I wasn't giving it to her. She was like all the other hypes by the corner store, begging. She didn't like my answer, so she slammed the door in my face.

It startled me, and I stumbled backward and fell to the ground. The little kids looked shocked and all ran over to me. I got up and kept walking, embarrassed and mad.

"That lady always act like that," one of them said.

"She a crackhead," another added.

I walked away slowly, looking out the gate and noticing how low 4946 had been chopped down since that day they started working on it at the beginning of spring. The closer they got to finishing that building meant our time was running out, and we'd have to leave. This fact put me in a terrible mood. My body felt the gravity of sadness and worry for my friend who was missing.

I tried to walk back down to the third floor, but I felt so tired. I looked over at the elevator; there was no way I was getting on there alone. I knew what happened to girls in there. That's when I thought about Stacia, remembering how when I'd first noticed her, she was in the elevator. I missed her, so I turned around and started walking *up* the stairs. She was mad at me, but I was going to her apartment anyway.

TWELVE

1502

R ight before I got to 1502, where all those Buchanans lived, I slowed down. I was getting scared. Who would answer the door? And what would Stacia say to me when she saw me? I didn't really have a plan, but I needed her, so I knocked. Jet, the baby of the family, was the only human walking around so early in the morning. His little voice asked, "Who is it?" I could imagine him arching shoulders back, pushing his chest forward to sound bigger.

"Fe Fe," I said, then added, "for Stacia." He opened the door.

"She sleep. Want me to get her?" Before I could decide what to tell him, he was halfway down the hall that led to their room. It's how he got the nickname Jet. I still don't know that boy's real name. I stood there a second, unsure whether or not I should go in. I peeked around the corner and decided I would, but stopped when I saw her brother, Sweat, knocked out, most of his body on the couch, but an uncomfortable amount hanging off. He wasn't wearing a shirt and had on these boxer shorts. I could see his erection straining against the fabric.

That's when I regretted walking in their apartment, but it was too late. I turned to leave but was too fascinated by everything in their living room. On the wall were velvet pictures in rich colors of Black people as kings and queens and Black people dancing at some old-time party and naked Black people just standing around in nature. I was confused when I felt sensations between my legs.

I glanced back over at Sweat, and the lump poking against his shorts. I took in the rest of his body. His chest strong, like something you could break glass over. He had arms that looked like somebody drew them. His legs, sculptures falling off the couch. I wouldn't forget this image for years; Sweat Buchanan was the first boy I ever had dreams about. My body warmed all of a sudden.

There was a long bar counter in the living room. It looked as if somebody would show up and ask me if I wanted a drink. The Buchanans had just as many bottles of alcohol as Food & Liquor. I hopped up on one of the stools and sat there, stealing glances at Sweat, hoping he wouldn't wake up and catch me being a creep.

I could hear Jet in the back of the apartment trying to wake up Stacia. "Stace!" He whined. "Yo' friend here for you," he sang out, sounding more and more pitiful every time he repeated it. The electric hum of the refrigerator and Sweat's breath coming out in gusts every once in a while served as music to his lyrics. Jet's pleas started waking up the rest of the house. Moon's feet swept the floor, and she came down the hallway, adding to the song. As she got closer to the living room, I started to panic, feeling guilty for sitting in her brother's bedroom and looking at his body like that.

"Hey, Fe Fe," she said, her voice raspy because she'd just gotten up.

I said, "Hey," in a smaller voice, trying my best not to wake Sweat.

She went in the bathroom and locked the door. I heard someone else coming down the hall, the steps too heavy to be another
small kid. It was Gail, Stacia's mama. I could hear her thumb skip-
ping on a lighter, and then it stopped, and so did her footsteps. She
didn't see me right away and went straight toward the bathroom.
Banging on the door, she said, with a cigarette pinched between
the edge of her lips, "Hurry the hell up! Gotta shit." She stood
there, out of my line of sight.

Jet ran by her and burst into the living room with an update.
"She won't get up."

"Okay," I said, breaking my neck to leave. I was really scared
of Stacia's mama, convinced she knew I was watching her son
sleep. I hadn't ever been this close to Gail. She was this massive
woman, the originator of the Buchanan face and head. She seemed
to always be upset about something. I found out, though, that her
smile didn't inspire warmth either.

I could feel her looking at me, so I turned around. Her mouth
curled up in a half smile around a cigarette. It smelled so nasty.
Smoke swirled around her, filling up the space between the kitchen
and the living room.

"Your mama know you up here?"

I remembered that Mama knew the Buchanans' phone number. My heart started beating fast because all she needed to do
was call Mama, and I would be in so much trouble. I didn't get to
lie, though, because she continued.

"She know you up in Gail Buchanan's apartment?"

She asked the question, and then started laughing. The laugh
ended with a cough that vibrated the phlegm in her throat. She
put a hand on the cabinet and bent a little, coughing. When she
got herself together, she said, wiping her eyes, "So you hang out
with Stace?"

I nodded. I had been hanging out with *Stace* almost as soon as she transferred to Farren earlier that year. Gail made a sound, looked me up and down, and walked away.

Moon finally left the bathroom, and Gail went in, commenting on how bad it smelled in there. Sweat hadn't moved, but Stacia's older sisters Pumpkin and Peach were now up and trying to get into the bathroom too. They looked funny: Peach's ponytail leaned to the side, her gelled baby hairs all smashed and crooked, eye makeup smudged. Pumpkin's hair was wrapped around like a beehive, clipped with a million bobby pins.

There were ten people in that apartment, with one bathroom. I tried not to stare, but I couldn't believe that so many people could live in one place. Doors were opening and closing, people were yelling across halls. Still no sign of life from Sweat. Gail left the bathroom and went back into the kitchen. Peach and Pumpkin were fighting to get into the bathroom next. Peach pushed Pumpkin into the wall, making a loud thud, but no one stopped to check on her. Gail didn't try to break up the fight. Instead, while moving some pots and pans around, and balancing that same cigarette on her bottom lip, she said, "You look just like your damned daddy."

My mouth eased open in shock. She let out a bark of laughter, and it shook her cigarette again.

"You knew my daddy?"

"Everybody knew your daddy," she said, and started laughing again, then coughing. "Shit, Stan was almost your daddy."

"Stan?"

"Stan Brown. He got a little girl your age. Special? Unique? What's that girl's name?"

"Precious," Stacia said, coming into the living room and leaning on the edge of the bar. "Yeah, her daddy." I looked at Gail with my mouth still open. My stomach felt like it was going to shrivel up like a raisin. She laughed, then said, "You didn't know that, huh? Janice and Stan. Ask your mama."

Before I could say anything else, Stacia's voice boomed behind me, asking, "What you want?" I looked back to see her annoyed facial expression. She had a hand on her hip and an eyebrow up. I knew I only had a few minutes to fix things.

"Can we go on the porch?"

We walked outside, and I said, "Bye, Ms. Buchanan," because I thought that I was supposed to.

"Ms. Buchanan?" she repeated, then laughed so hard, she fell into another coughing spell. I looked over at Sweat one last time. Nothing had changed. If it wasn't for his chest moving up and down, you might think he wasn't even alive.

On the porch, Stacia turned her attitude all the way up. "What?" she asked, her arms crossed, hair looking a mess. You couldn't tell if it used to be in a ponytail or not.

"My brother Folks now," I said, sad, my shoulders hanging low.

"I know," she said. She went over to the gate, pressed her face against it, as if she were looking for him. I walked over there too, leaned close to the gate but careful not to let my face touch the iron. We looked down there at his new home. She seemed to get lost in thought, so we stayed quiet for a moment.

"Can you help me get him back?" I said, stepping away from the gate. She moved back too, her face full of diamonds from the impression of the iron.

"Back?" She stared at me like I was the dumbest thing she'd ever seen. "You such a baby, Fe Fe."

She was laughing at me and walking away. Anger took over my body, and I felt hot again. I screamed, "Didn't nobody call you a hoe when you was in the elevator with that dude."

She snatched her body around and stared at me. She looked so crazy with the gate shapes on her face and how mad she was. Like an animal crouching low, getting a good look at you first. Stacia seemed to rev up, then leaped at me! I wasn't ever the cutest girl in the room, and I've only come close to being the smartest, but everybody at school and even people back at the building knew that you couldn't catch me for nothing.

I darted down the stairs, and she chased me, screaming things at me, trying to hurt my feelings. "Your brother one of us now, bitch!" was the most hurtful one.

I had a whole floor of a lead on her, and as I barreled through the stairwell onto the eighth floor, she called out, "And we gone fuck that hoe up, watch!"

I thought it was an idle threat. I didn't think about the "we" that she mentioned, and I didn't believe she'd beat up Tonya, but what I didn't realize was that Stacia was growing up fast, and that summer, she'd gotten tired of playing kid games with me and Precious, and that she wanted so desperately to be more like her big sisters. I had no clue just how far she'd go to gain their approval and step into her place as a Buchanan gangster.

THIRTEEN

The Elevator

Around the first week of our sixth-grade school year, something happened to Stacia. It still doesn't make much sense to me, how I just happened to be with her at the time. It was the weekend. Mama sent me to the store with her Link card and a list as long as my arm, so the bag was heavier than usual. When I got through the breezeway and saw that the elevator door was still open, I ran on, even though it was packed; there was even a boy with a ten-speed bike. I slid into a small space. When I think back to that day, I don't really know why I got in the elevator. But a couple years later, when I am a teenager, the superstitious side of me will run wild, and I will remember the moment as something spiritual, as if God nudged me toward the open door, led me into that metal box.

Once in the elevator, I asked if someone could press three. So many people kissed their teeth, it sounded like the intro to a rap song. Someone summed up the sounds, and said, "Shit, you could've walked."

No one pressed my floor, and when the doors opened, I was

on the nine. I stepped off the elevator to let people out, and before I walked back on, I looked over at the stairs. I could've run
down them, but I decided to get back on. I didn't look around at
who was in the elevator because even today, most adult elevator
etiquette seems to suggest you never make eye contact in small
spaces. When the doors opened again on the ten, this old lady
took her sweet time walking off. The boy with the bike left too.

I was starting to get nervous then, because Mama timed my
trips to the store, and I worried that she would know that this
one took too long. We shifted around again, and that's when I
saw a girl my age with that Buchanan head, her hair slicked over
in a side ponytail. But this girl wasn't standing all confident like
the Stacia I would soon become friends with. She wasn't popping
gum; she was scared. I didn't know her well at the time—she was
just a kid in my class who everybody was afraid of because her
family ran the gang on our block.

The elevator left the tenth floor and went express all the way
up to sixteen. Its doors didn't even open. It dropped back down to
the nine, like some ride at Six Flags. Everybody started cursing.
I looked over at the corner where the girl was, but I couldn't see
her well; most of her body was covered up by this man who had
her face pressed against the elevator wall. It was bizarre, especially since there was elbow room now. I couldn't stop staring at
them. At first, it looked like a couple getting it on in the elevator,
something you'd see, then look away from, which is, I know now,
how so many public assaults happen.

When the door opened on seven, everyone else had had
enough, and hurried off, cursing about the elevator. I stayed on
and as I looked closer to see if she was Stacia, I realized the guy
was a grown man, and that while he seemed calm, the girl was
not enjoying herself. She was crying.

I knew she was in danger, but then I started doubting what I was looking at. I couldn't hear what he was saying, but he mumbled something in her ear, not paying any attention to what the elevator was doing. He hadn't turned around once since I'd noticed them. I moved to get a closer look at the girl, who struggled to get her face off the elevator wall, and that's when I saw that she was Stacia for sure.

I didn't think before I pushed his shoulder as hard as I could and said, "Leave her alone!"

He spun around and reached for me. The next thing I knew, I was falling, then sliding down the metal wall into a trash pile of potato chip bags and candy wrappers on the elevator floor. He stared down at me, and said, "Mind your fucking business." Stacia looked at me, her face rippling with fear. When the door opened on six, he walked off, then looked back at Stacia with a little smile before walking away. I slipped on sticky dirt, trying to get up. We were the only two people in that box, and all you could hear was the elevator moving down, a rattling like a metal snake.

Stacia buttoned her pants with shaky fingers, her face completely wet from tears. I wanted to ask her if she was okay, but I knew she wasn't. I thought about rubbing her back like Mama did when I cried, but I figured she'd hit me. I didn't know what to do. The door opened on five, and this other man tried to get on before Stacia could get off, but she pushed past him. I ran off too.

On the way downstairs, I felt sorry for what just happened to her. I paused and looked up through the stairway rails and saw a small hand sliding up the banister.

———

THE NEXT DAY, WHEN I saw her in the school cafeteria for break-fast, she looked embarrassed and snatched her head away try-ing to stay tough. I wasn't scared anymore. She was becoming a whole person, someone who could be hurt, a kid who had feelings, like me.

I wondered if she was acting all tough because she had prob-lems back at the building. I didn't know if she had to deal with that man all the time. That's when I had the thought that maybe she needed some friends.

I called her name, and she turned around and looked at me, but instantly, I could tell that she felt shame and didn't want to talk to me. "My name Fe Fe, your name Stacia, right?" It was stupid; we knew each other's names from attendance.

"Yeah," she said, looking away and putting her head down a little.

"That's Precious," I said, looking back and pointing toward Precious seated at another table. She knew that too. "We play rope on the three. Can you jump?"

THAT'S WHAT I THOUGHT ABOUT on the way down the stairs after running from Stacia, figuring that it was all for nothing, that now, we'd never be friends again, because she thought that I was teasing her for what that man did to her in the elevator. I guess it didn't come out right, so our lives from then on would be just like our hands on those banisters: moving fast in opposite directions.

FOURTEEN

301

After outrunning Stacia, something strange started happening by the time I got to the seventh floor. It was like what I saw got blotted out by white lights, and then I missed a step, slid down a few more, and landed at the bottom of the stairs. I was on my feet, but still unbalanced. I stood up straight, but everything looked cloudy, like I was in a dream. I tried to walk down the rest of the stairs, really looking at each foot placement, but the world continued to appear hazy.

I started to worry that maybe I was high. Stacia always talked about contact highs, and how if you breathed in the weed in the air, you could feel it. I didn't think weed made you dizzy, but I didn't really know. When I got to the third floor, I looked down the porch at my door, but went the other way. I didn't feel well, like my breakfast was on its way up. I wanted my brother in that moment, someone safe and comforting. If Mama saw me, she'd ask me too many questions, and I'd let something slip about the Buchanans and be in trouble.

I got the idea to go down to Mama Pearl's. Mama Pearl was

a lot like my grandma who had died before I was in kindergarten, though I never treated her like my grandma. She was more like an aunt, but that's not quite right either. That summer, she became my friend. I could count on her to tell me things, real things, to hold nothing back.

You couldn't get Mama Pearl to talk bad about Grandma, but I knew that she hated my grandfather and how Grandma got married and stopped talking to her for a long time. Mama Pearl still wore wigs that had the same hairstyle Grandma had in all her pictures. They even talked the same, saying things like "Baby, retch around that chair and gimme a blanket," or "I reckon so," instead of "Yes."

It was Saturday afternoon, and I knew she'd be home from church, napping or sitting in her recliner. Just like Grandma, she grew up Seventh-day Adventist, so her holy day was Friday night to Saturday night. When you went to her house between those times, she'd let you in, but you couldn't turn on the TV or get her to take you to the store. She sat there with her Bible or little books about God. If you were quiet long enough, she'd start humming a church hymn.

I knew what I was walking into. It wasn't bad; it just wasn't what we did in my house. After Grandma died, Mama stopped going to church, so God was a big mystery to me.

Meechie remembered. He told me that one time, in Sabbath school, the teacher gave out toys, and he got a tiny Transformer. That's his strongest memory of church; that somebody gave him the perfect gift.

I tried to fix my face before I got to her door, to straighten up before I knocked. She opened the door, and I must've looked bad, because she asked, "What's the matter, Chile?" I opened my mouth, then closed it and just stood on the other side of the frame looking up at her face, but the little white lights had blurred it.

"Come on in here, you letting the heat in," she said, holding the door open for me.

I walked inside and told her, "I don't feel good."

She came over to me and put the back of her hand on my forehead. "You hot!" she said. "Gone sit down."

I took a seat on the couch and closed my eyes to stop the room from spinning. I heard house shoes moving in the other direction, and water running, ice clinking, then shoes brushing the tile again. Things were still twirling, and I could see the lights dancing back and forth.

"Drink. And put this on your head," she said, handing me a makeshift ice pack. She sat in silence for only a few seconds before asking, "Where you coming from?"

Older people always seem to know the unspoken. They can sense when you've been doing something dangerous. They know when you need help and haven't asked for it. I didn't even try to lie.

"I went to see Stacia."

"Went to *see* her?!" When I didn't explain myself, she said, "You stay 'way from 'round there."

It was too much work to say or do anything, so I just kept my eyes closed, sucking on the ice.

"Drink that up, then you lay down. I'll tell your mama you here." She got up again and went in the kitchen to grab her phone off of the wall.

That's all I remember. When I woke up, I felt funny, but the room had stopped rotating, and the dancing white lights were gone.

Mama Pearl had fallen asleep too. I could hear the fan making breathing noises, but it hadn't cooled the room down. When I tried to get up and leave, Mama Pearl's eyes popped open.

I flopped back down, and my thoughts went back to my brother.

"Meechie," I said, low, and then I stopped talking and started playing with a hangnail. "He in trouble" was all that I could say. She just looked at me.

"In trouble how?" I couldn't say the words. I looked up at her, then out the window. She didn't need an answer, though. She just asked me, "Do he even want your help?"

I looked back at her and hunched my shoulders. "Somebody need to help him, Mama Pearl," I said, and then I came really close to crying.

"Come here, Chile," she said, and opened her arms. I left the couch, the plastic making a sucking sound as it released my legs. She hugged me and said, "I'm gone pray for that boy, you hear? I'm gone give this to God, and I need you to let it go. Ain't much you can do. You a kid. He is too, but, baby, chil'ren don't get to be chil'ren no mo'."

I moved my face from her arm and looked at her.

"Can I pray for him too?"

"You show can." Even though she didn't know the details, I felt like we were doing something.

In the middle of our sad moment, outside her window, I heard voices of kids calling to each other and playing, and I thought about what Mama Pearl just said, about how no one gets to be a child anymore. I started crying. Mama Pearl wouldn't let this be. She came back with a lecture that I wasn't in the mood to hear.

"You run around trying to take care of that boy like you done birthed him."

"He my brother," I told her.

"If you ain't careful, you'll be doing it your whole life. One day, you'll have yo'self a little boyfriend, and you'll try to mother him too. And don't get married! You'll think you got a right to run after him, wiping his nose." She took a deep breath and said, "Your brother act a lot like his daddy. They gotta go out into the world and try everything. You can't tell 'em nothing. Sometimes, the thangs they try ruin their lives forever. You gone have to let your brother make his own choices."

I wanted to ask her more about our dad. It seemed like everybody knew him except for me. She kept talking, though, and mostly she wanted me to stay out of Meechie's way, and I knew that I wouldn't.

"I gotta go," I said.

"Oh, now you gots to go?"

"My mama—"

"You hear what I say, now."

I nodded, but I had to leave. The GDs had Meechie. They'd taken him from me. I wasn't about to listen to her tell me that I couldn't help. Back then, I believed if you wanted it enough, you could save anybody. My basic understanding of salvation would cause me to be at odds with God in those early days of our relationship.

I went to the door and looked back at her. She was up again, following me so that she could lock it and put the chain back on.

"He done joined that gang," she said. "You gone have to let him go." Her words slid down my sweaty back, and I left them on the porch by her screen door.

FIFTEEN

304

I was feeling weird again. Air curled in the back of my throat, and the lighting of the porch seemed odd, like I was watching a flashback scene in a movie. The colors went matte, and I saw everything through a haze. I planned to go home, but I didn't think I could make it without falling. I stumbled a few feet down the porch to where Precious lived, holding on to the brick wall. Over the years, her place had become a second home. I could hear a whole group of ladies in there Amening and Yes-Lording and Thank-you-Jesusing. Their voices bounced out the open window.

I knew what it was like to show up to 304 on a Saturday afternoon, that there would be a Bible Study, but something was still wrong with me, and after leaving Mama Pearl's, it seemed like the safest place to go.

I leaned into their door and knocked. Ms. Patty, Precious's mama, opened it. "Felicia! Come in!" she said. I walked in the living room, and five women sat around the couches, dressed all fancy. Everybody's skin glossed from sweat, so they waved themselves with paper fans on wooden sticks. Precious was there too, with her own fan. She looked up to the women sitting there in the circle. Later that summer, after she was baptized, she'd strive to stay on a path to become as devoted and holy.

Ms. Patty pointed to a spot by this lady wearing a purple suit. I squeezed in next to her, feeling like I was going to fall over. About three different strong scents floated around that tiny room: the perfume Ms. Patty always wore, a high-pitched floral scent; the one the lady next to me took a bath in; and bleach from the floor tiles. This combination wasn't making me any less nauseated.

"I'm so glad you came by, Felicia. It's not too early to start thinking about your salvation," Ms. Patty said. I didn't know what that meant and was starting to get scared because the room twirled around again, the white light returning and the feeling in my throat getting stronger; I worried that I would throw up all over these ladies and their nice clothes.

"Precious, you want to introduce Felicia?" Ms. Patty said.

"This is Felicia Stevens. She's my best friend," Precious told them.

They thought that was the sweetest thing, so they all started to talk, saying things like "Welcome, Felicia!" and "Oh!" and when they calmed down, Ms. Patty said, "Sister Greer was just giving us her testimony."

She picked up where she left off, as if I really came by to join them. I stared at my hands while she talked, then looked over at Precious without raising my head. She stared at the lady, her cheeks rosy and sweet, so I looked around the circle at everybody, bouncing my knee, searching for a face I could trust. Precious wouldn't make eye contact, but then I saw this lady whose hair was definitely a wig, and whose skin was perfectly clear, except for a few dots of moles. She kept glancing at me and could tell something was wrong.

I stopped bouncing my knee and looked back at her. She interrupted Sister Greer and said, "Baby, is there something you need to talk about?"

My eyes widened and shot around the group. I thought about Meechie giving that handshake. My heart bumped in my chest, and sweat dripped from my hairline. More white lights, shaped like lightning bolts, danced in front of me, floating by slowly like bubbles, until I couldn't see anybody clearly, their faces all blotted out by white.

I frowned at this new, lovely scene, and some of the women leaned forward and some of them encouraged me, saying, "It's alright, you're safe here," but I didn't understand what was happening, and I tried to talk and tell them that I needed their help, that I was feeling sick and couldn't stop worrying about Tonya and Meechie. I closed my eyes and gave in to the spinning. I heard high heels clicking on the tile and running water. Precious squatted down in front of me, her little voice trying to cheer me up, but I talked over her, slow and slurred like Woody after he's killed a few bottles of Night Train. Someone put a cup to my lips, but that's all that I remember.

I woke up in the Browns' car, moving dangerously fast. Voices knocked against voices, and I could smell Mama in there, cherry lotion and baby powder. When I came to, I looked into Meechie's eyes. I thought it was a dream, even though I could feel his breath on my arm. When I reached up for him and felt his white tee, it confirmed that he was there.

I didn't understand why I was in the Browns' Camry, so I started losing it, trying to ask questions. Meechie put his hand on my shoulder, and I stopped moving. He said, "You gone be okay."

"Meechie," I said through tears.

"I'm here." I shook my head and cried, calling his name again.

"What, Fee?"

"You gone move back?"

He looked away from my face, out the car window. I knew that he'd just said no, and I passed out again.

SIXTEEN

Sanctuary

At the hospital, the doctor told me that I was severely dehydrated, but also suffering from a migraine. I hit her with a million questions because I'd never even heard the word *migraine* before. She explained it to me, but said that she didn't know why I got them in the first place, that it could be worry or certain scents or a number of other things that triggered them.

This terrified me. I couldn't imagine a life where every time I even *thought* about something negative, my head would start to feel like it would crack open.

But the doctor just told me to take it easy, and Mama nodded. She had a plan to help me calm down; she'd make me attend church all week with the Browns. This would be my life until I started high school and replaced some of the church groups with things that I chose.

Precious spent most of her childhood at the New Hope Seventh-day Adventist Church in Hyde Park, where her mama flexed her bubbly personality and the church members worshipped her dad, who was the first elder. In small churches, this position had a ton of weight, since the first elder preached and ran the church when the pastor couldn't be there. Her daddy's family, the Browns, and Mama's family, the Stevens, go way back to Jackson, Mississippi. We had this friendship our mothers put together, even though I found out that summer that they never really liked one another. Gail was right; my mama and Precious's father used to date when they were students at DuSable. He met Ms. Patty at Oakwood University, then brought her back to Chicago. They didn't want their kids associating with "project kids," so they gritted their teeth and planned our playdates, putting their personal issues aside.

At first, I thought the Browns were crazy for going to church so much, and on Saturdays, not Sundays. And now, I couldn't understand why Mama would make me go with them on a day cartoons ran all morning long, *good* cartoons too. It wasn't even just church. I had to sing in the choir—that practice was on Friday nights—and attend prayer meeting on Wednesday evenings. Then she signed me up for the Pathfinder Club, a coed scout-like group that met on Sunday mornings. As if this wasn't enough, at the end of July, the church erected this circus-size tent outside and had a service every weeknight! I felt like I was being punished, so I tried to hate it.

Then something happened. On one of those Saturdays that Mr. Brown had to preach, we all piled into the Browns' navy-blue car at five forty-five in the morning. There wasn't one crackhead outside, no one selling drugs or candy; it was so early, the sun hadn't even come up yet. By this time, I'd been in the church on several occasions, but never so early in the morning. You could still see some of the pinks and oranges lingering in the sky. I sat in the back seat in stiff church clothes that originally seemed like part of the punishment but I'd secretly grown to like. Both Precious *and* her mother had on too much of that perfume, and I worried that I might get another migraine. These loud scents were the same perfumes that I smelled the first time I got a migraine a few weeks before. I hadn't felt anything weird since, but I feared that I'd see those white lights dancing again.

We got to the church in about seven minutes. Mr. Brown pulled out a bundle of keys, and something about this made me realize that church is just a building. It looked pretty dingy in the dusk of morning, kind of sad. The paint peeled in some places, and without the elders to greet you at the door or all the cars and people laughing and talking in the parking lot, the whole scene was almost scary.

The windows had stained glass art, but in the dark, they didn't look so special. The maroon, navy, and mustard colors just looked like poor choices by whoever made the windows. Mr. Brown opened the huge front doors, and I twisted my lips and rolled my eyes. I wanted my peanut butter Cap'n Crunch and *The Bugs Bunny and Tweety Show.*

Inside, the Browns flipped on secret switches, and slowly the lights grew stronger. Then this old, grumpy man appeared seconds later, and started the air-conditioning. Watching them start up the church only proved my point: it was all a lie.

Mr. Brown dipped off to his study, and Mrs. Brown went to prepare for her Sabbath school class, then Precious grabbed my hand and pulled me up the stairs. She opened the doors to the sanctuary, and we walked in slow and respectfully. She headed down the center aisle, but I hung back and looked around in the almost dark, noticing that the ceilings were nearly as high as the fourth floor of our building. There were two columns of wide benches with at least thirty rows and a stage running the length of both sides. It was a lot to take in.

Precious stood still, looking at those ugly-colored windows. She waved me over instead of talking. Before I got to her, it happened: the sun blazed through the first few stained glass panels, and the blues, reds, and gold colors lightened around three angels in the middle of each one.

The angels had these white robes on, and their faces warmed to various brown complexions and you could see their afros, blond, red, and black. They blew into bronze trumpets tilted in the air. I could feel the heat as the sunlight, sharp like lasers, zipped through the pews.

Precious looked back at me with the biggest smile, the shock on my face making her laugh. She turned around and walked up a few places before sitting down.

I just stood there in the middle of the sanctuary. It wasn't just the sun, and the life it gave that room. I felt something else; God seemed to speak through that light and those windows. A calm took over me, and I was no longer angry about being there.

God was somehow in those colors, I'd discover, in the quiet. I slipped into the pew closest to me and sat at the corner. When I looked up at Precious, she seemed to be praying, so I bowed my head too.

I thought about how, as a girl in Mississippi, Mama spent all week in church. She came from generations of Seventh-day Adventists and was active in this church until she got pregnant with Meechie. She wasn't married to my dad, and people judged her, so she left the church. I'd learn that months away from church turn into years very easily, and just like Mama, after getting close to church, I'd lose my way from the sanctuary as well. We'd both return, though, and the Browns would be there to welcome us back to those same pews, with the same stained glass angels blowing their trumpets.

I sat there with my eyes closed, then I heard the doors creaking. I took a peek and saw Ms. Patty. She walked down the side aisle closest to the windows and sat at a bench far away from Precious—who still hadn't lifted her head or opened her eyes. Ms. Patty lowered her head and didn't move. I closed my eyes again and kept them shut as the door opened two more times. We sat there, not saying a word. Then suddenly Mr. Brown started talking out loud, a prayer for us all, and everyone said, all together, "Amen." It was how they got ready to run church.

When Mr. Brown preached, we came to church early and did the same thing. Something about praying made me breathe easier. By the time we said amen, I felt like I had just gotten up from a good night's sleep. Sitting quiet like that was new to me.

In our neighborhood, the only time you could have some peace and quiet was between the hours of four and six o'clock in the morning. Four was about the time that the last of the gang members on duty went to bed. Six was just before the crackheads started roaming the block like zombies, looking for somebody to sell them something. Our block always had voices on top of voices, talking or screaming or somebody calling a kid to come home or a friend to come to them, their names echoing around the playgrounds and parking lot.

Sometimes there were dogs barking or planes in the sky or a motorcycle zooming down State Street. In our apartment, Mama kept the radio or TV on. There was nowhere in my life I could just be quiet except in church. It didn't take but a minute before I was hooked. Eventually, I learned that you could find quiet anywhere. I started doing it at home, early in the mornings, when both Mama and the block were still asleep. I wanted to hate church, but I failed. The things that I liked piled up so fast. It started with the dresses and shiny, clicking shoes. There was no place I could dress like that.

At church, people tried to be nice to you, wished you well, and gave you hugs. These men hung out at the door to say "Happy Sabbath" to people coming in. They dressed in suits, and their smiles didn't drip with nasty thoughts. They were the grandpas that I never had. Even though I was young, they still called me Sister. "How you doing, Sister?" and "Happy Sabbath, Sister."

Every time I went to church, it was like I paused what was going wrong in my life. No one talked about the Robert Taylor Homes. We talked about God: What God had done that past week. What God said God would do for us. We praised God just because. We looked for God in each other. At church, we looked up for so long, that when we came back down to our lives, we felt stronger to deal with the mess.

That's why I *knew* I could save Meechie, because I'd have God to help me. For the longest time, I had such a simplistic idea of what it meant to save. You'd hear it all week: *Jesus saves.* You'd read it everywhere. I was praying and going to church, so you couldn't tell me that Jesus wouldn't give me what I asked for.

ONE OF THE BEST THINGS about New Hope, I found, was that they fed you after the service. In the church basement, these ladies worked like elves, whipping up pasta dishes and bread that always seemed warm and ready for butter.

I sat across from Mr. Brown and looked at him as he held court, his voice thick and layered like most pastors, yet mellow enough so that kids weren't afraid of him. Gail said he could've been my dad, and that meant only one thing: that Mr. Brown,

Stan, was once Mama's boyfriend. I couldn't imagine it, though. I watched him eat and talk, and I pretended to listen, but what I really tried to imagine was what he would've been like as my father. Was he a nice man behind closed doors? And how did having a dad at home change things? I thought about Uncle Tim and Auntie Nora, and how Mama seemed more intense and stressed than her sister. I imagined Mr. Brown as Mama's uncle Tim and thought that maybe if he had been my father, it would've been okay.

SEVENTEEN

Plans

The next morning was a Sunday, which meant I'd spend hours on the floor getting my hair done. After Mama finished, I hopped up right away and went down the porch to get Precious. I didn't really feel like jumping rope; I just wanted to talk. We dragged out chairs and sat on the porch, facing the gate so that we could look into the playground. Sometimes, it was nice to do nothing like this, to sit, think, talk. Precious and I had a rhythm that we'd perfected over our twelve years of life, and I think that her friendship that summer helped me make it through the toughest days. I couldn't ever sit like this with Stacia because she wasn't a great listener and she dismissed my feelings. I rarely had time alone with Tonya, and on the few occasions that we were by ourselves, I mostly asked her questions about her very mysterious life.

When Precious and I were in kindergarten, we'd hang out on the school playground, and instead of climbing and jumping or playing rope with the other girls, sometimes, we'd just sit and look around, asking questions about life. Right around that time, when we started school at Farren, our families put their differences aside and let us have playdates, visiting each other's apartments. After all these years, I knew her place as well as mine: every linen closet, where the good snacks were hidden in the cabinets, where to grab toilet paper if I'd finished the roll. And she could hang at my place, pulling books off the shelf and taking out the bookmark that she'd placed there, knowing that she couldn't read Stephen King or my Sweet Valley High books at her house.

I'll never forget, though, how the first time Precious came over to visit, Mama put her out. It was a misunderstanding. Mama thought Precious was being rude, but she was just a shy kid who went for a bowl of lemon drops without asking.

Mama used to think that Precious was spoiled, spent too much time "sitting under grown folks," and would be a handful once she was older, but over the years, she saw how well we got along and looked out for each other, and later, I'd catch her smiling at us. Precious won her over.

On the porch that day, I asked Precious about moving.

"We got our voucher meeting in a few weeks," she said. I gave her a confused frown. "If you Lease Compliant, they send you a letter about a meeting. After the meeting, you can start looking for a new place. Then you move."

I felt my breathing change. Precious was going to leave me, after all those years; she was going to live somewhere else and I couldn't even imagine how that would work.

"Where you moving to?"

She hunched her shoulders, and we just stared at each other.

"My mother said that you and I would still see each other."

I nodded but worried that Ms. Patty would take this opportunity to remove me from Precious's life and fill it with other church kids and cousins and friends whose mothers didn't have such a personal relationship with her husband.

I looked through the gate into the playground and wondered how anyone could go about their day like everything wasn't about to be ripped out from under us. Precious cut into my thoughts and asked, "What your mama planning?"

I felt the sting in my eyes. This was a sore subject for me. Mama had plans, I was sure of it, but she hadn't shared any of them with me. Why did the Browns have a letter telling them to come to a meeting? Were we even Lease Compliant? I still didn't know.

She saw the shine in my eyes and realized that I'd paused too long to be okay, and she started rubbing my back and saying, "God won't leave you, Fee. It's gonna all work out." She was right, it *was* a good time to pray and have faith, but I didn't feel strong enough to lean on God like that. I decided, instead, to panic. Precious delivered a second blow when she told me, "I'm getting baptized in a few weeks." It was the biggest commitment you could make to God, and she was doing it at twelve. I had just gotten used to going to church. Precious made me feel like I wasn't serious about life; in that one summer, she'd make some pretty big decisions, while I dragged my feet. I had plans and wishes and hopes too. I'd written them all down in my journal.

"My daddy committed his life to God at the same age."

"What's your daddy really like?" I asked, maybe a bit too fast. Before she could even answer, her face flushed red, bloomed really, slow and lovely like a flower bursting out of a bud. That was love. That's how kids loved their parents when they were around and spent time with them and invested in them. That smile made me jealous. I didn't even know who my father was, where he was, and if he even thought about me at all. And here she was so overwhelmed with emotion that she couldn't even answer my questions. She finally said, "My dad is present and sweet, and he want to help everybody."

"Present?"

"When he's with you, you got his attention."

I liked her answer. I pushed my face against the gate, let it move through me for a while.

I peered into the world as if I was searching for my dad. Then Precious said, "But he works all the time, and I wish I could see him more. I know it's the Lord's work, but sometimes, I don't want to share my dad with the whole world."

I pulled my face off the gate and looked at her. She wasn't crying, but she looked sad. I didn't know what to say, so I just asked her, "You think you'll still be at church all the time after you move?"

"Yeah. After you get baptized, they put you to work!" We both laughed at how she said it. Then got quiet again. We listened to the sounds of the block, which always sounded like layered echoes of people calling to each other and laughter, mixed in with bass from someone's music. We were comfortable sitting in silence together, having our own thoughts that we'd share once they emerged or we'd keep to ourselves, but there was an ease with Precious that I didn't have with my other friends.

She scratched her arm, a nervous tic I'd noticed years before, so I asked her, "What you thinking about?

"Tonya," she said. "I worry that we haven't seen her because of those guys. Remember when she used to walk up and down the stairs all day, every day? Now it's like she's just gone."

"And every time I go up to her house, her mama say she ain't home."

"Fe Fe, it's been like three weeks since she been to the square." We were quiet again, then Precious said, "We really gotta pray for her."

Precious was right: Tonya needed our prayers, and Stacia

knew more than she was saying. But me and Stacia weren't even friends anymore. Everything was messed up, and I didn't know how to get us back to the way we were, like earlier in the summer, when we were just a group of girls, and I could fix things with hand games and cheers. Somehow, we were all growing apart; I could feel it, but chose to deny this truth.

EIGHTEEN

Salvation

As we crept toward the end of July, it was so hot that both sweat and conflict dripped nonstop. You couldn't find a breeze, just sun and ninety-degree weather and heat advisories, telling people to drink lots of water and stay in the house if they didn't have to go out. Since we were kids, we *had* to go out. Precious and I played rope with blue lips from freeze pops and drank water even though there was no sugar in it. We jumped with just two people again, like it was the earlier days of our friendship, which made me sad, but I knew we'd lost Stacia forever, and I didn't dare invite another stranger into the square.

After I was getting used to having just one friend around, Tonya returned. She'd been gone long enough to visit relatives in another state, like maybe she got a chance to see her daddy in Mississippi like she wanted. I couldn't wait to ask her where she'd been.

"My mama wouldn't let me come outside," she said, looking at her shoes. I knew right away that either she or her mama lied to me. I'd snuck up to the ten almost every day, knocking on her door. Sometimes Rochelle would swing the door open; sometimes there was no answer at all.

"You was on punishment?"

She shook her head no.

Precious asked, with a frown, "Then why you have to stay in the house that long?"

"Let's just play," Tonya said, grabbing the rope. And that's when I knew that maybe she wasn't telling us the truth. We started a game and let ourselves enjoy jumping, the exercise smoothing out the awkward tension, the game bringing us back to the joys of childhood. I missed Stacia, who was now spending all her time in the playground with her sisters. She dressed like an older girl with tighter, more revealing clothes and hair extensions. I thought that she'd just found a new friend circle with her sister and her sister's friends, and that she wasn't thinking about us anymore, but I was wrong.

The day that Tonya returned, as if they were tracking her movements, Stacia, her sisters Pumpkin and Peach, along with their friends Meka and Valencia, all came to the square looking for Tonya.

They ran from the other end of the porch, which gave us a head start. Even if those girls walked up slowly, eating snow cones, I would've still run. They all had a reputation for being just as ruthless as the dudes downstairs. We ran into the Browns' apartment. When the three of us got there, we locked the doors, then I screamed, "Get down!" because I didn't know if they had guns. We dropped to the floor and listened as they banged on the windows, then one of them said, "We just want that hoe!"

On the floor, we breathed hard in each other's faces. I looked at Tonya and asked, "Why them girls trying to kick your ass?" then put my hand over my mouth, since we were in the Browns' sanctuary of an apartment. I was trying my best to stop cursing.

Precious looked right up at Jesus hanging on the wall, then back at me, as if I knew better. She got up, ran to the back of her apartment to tell her parents what happened. I heard her back there crying and hiccuping her way through the story.

When Tonya hadn't answered, I asked again, "Why they chasing you?"

"Meka saw me in Nook's car."

"Doing what in Nook's car?" I asked.

She dropped her head, ashamed.

That's when I asked her, "Was you having sex with him?" All of Stacia's warnings and accusations started to make sense. She hadn't been making things up.

She started crying. I didn't know what to say then. I knew that was a yes. I looked around Precious's living room like I hadn't ever been in there before, thinking Stacia *was* right about Tonya.

Precious came back in the room with her parents. They checked to see if the girls were gone, then helped us up off of the floor. They immediately started talking about how bad the neighborhood had gotten, and how they're so ready to move. Precious, Tonya, and I sat in the living room quiet, not knowing what to do.

I looked back up at the cross, then asked Precious, "How Jesus get up on that cross?"

"They nailed him up there by his hands and feet."

Me and Tonya just looked at Precious, then back at Jesus.

Then Precious said, "They thought he was lying about being God."

Then her mother and father got all quiet in the kitchen, listening to us. Ms. Patty cut in.

"He did it to save us, Felicia." There it was again, all this talk about saving people, that no one would break down for me. Our entire neighborhood needed saving—our buildings, my brother, Tonya—and it didn't seem like any of it was being saved by Jesus. My literal interpretation of salvation was the reason I got so angry at God by the end of that fall. Later, I vowed not to sling these doctrines around so carelessly; it's easy for kids to take these words at face value, then get disappointed when things don't happen on the spot.

THE VERY NEXT DAY, I went back to Tonya's house to see if she could come outside. This time, she opened the door. Before I could say hi, she grabbed my arm and yanked me in. It was like a cave in there. There were no lights, and it was morning but already sweltering. When we talked, our voices bounced around the room, the echo of old words coming back smothering new ones.

"How come you ain't got no furniture?" I asked before thinking about how rude the question was.

Tonya looked away from me and then said, real low, "We used to have furniture."

"Somebody broke in your house?" I asked.

She shook her head from side to side.

"What happened?"

"The furniture company took it. Our other stuff, I don't know what happened to it. Sometimes, I come home from school, stuff just be gone. We moved over here with nothing but our beds and clothes." I couldn't say nothing. Before I could change the subject, and ask her how she been, she just kept talking. "It first started back when my little brothers and sister used to stay with us. I remember my mama telling us to stay in our room, and watch TV, and to not come out for nothing. We did stay in our room, but one time, I had to pee, and I opened the door, and I thought something was on fire, cause it smelled like something was burning. I went in the front room, and Mama was laying on the couch like she was real sleepy. Her eyes half opened. I walk closer to look at her, and then I saw this pipe laying on the couch. I went back to my room and Devon, Mina, and Mikey ain't even know I left cause they was staring at the TV."

"Them your brothers and sister?" I asked.

She nodded.

I tried to stay calm but was getting excited by how much she was saying to me.

"They daddy took them," she told me, and she wasn't crying or nothing, and I wondered what could make a kid get chased by girls who probably had guns and razors or get dragged off by grown men or live without her brothers and sister and not cry every single day. I didn't ask anything else; I just let her talk.

"Every time Mama told us to stay in our room, I knew that she was smoking that pipe. I started to hear voices in the living room. Then the TV was gone. One day, I came out of the room, walked down the hall, and looked. People was all over our living room, looking like Mama did that day, and she wasn't even in the house.

"Some of them was people from downstairs, crackheads that I had seen scratching and looking crazy around my building. That's when I knew that she was on that stuff. I ran back to the room and closed the door. My heart was beating so fast, I thought my chest was gone blow up. After that, things started changing. Furniture started leaving the house. We ain't never have no food in the re-frigerator."

"How do you eat?" I asked.

"At school."

"That's the only food you get? At lunchtime?"

She shook her head from side to side. "I go to breakfast too."

"You can eat at my house, Tonya," I said. "Anytime you want to."

"Okay," she said. "Thank you."

And after that thank you I asked, "If your mama on drugs, who taught you manners?"

She hunched her shoulders and smiled. She looked so pretty and innocent, and it broke my heart that my friend had this life.

"She wasn't always on drugs. She used to work and be nice and stuff, but she changed. She would tell me and my sister and brothers to be nice to people even if they mean to you, and say 'thank you' and 'excuse me' and 'please.' And she ain't take no stuff from nobody, but now, she act like a little kid. People talk to her any kind of way, and the drug dealers, even though some of them ain't nothing but sixteen, she let them say anything to her, and sometimes—" She stopped and dropped her head.

"What?" I asked, leaning in.

"She do stuff to them."

"What kind of stuff?"

She looked down at her feet again, but then said, "Nasty stuff."

My eyes got big, and all that I could say was "For real?"

She nodded. "Then some of them came after me."

My mouth dropped open, and I thought about all the stuff that Stacia had said about Tonya knowing a bunch of dudes on the block, those boys dragging her out of the rope that day, and how she said she'd been caught in Nook's car, probably doing stuff to him.

"One day, on the way home from school, this man tell me to 'come here.' He say, 'What's yo' name?' and he asking me and looking all over me. I tell him, and then he say, 'Tonya, you got a boyfriend?' I tell him no, and then he say he want to be my boyfriend. I say, 'You grown!' cause he should know better than to try to go with a kid. 'No I'm not, I'm seventeen,' and even seventeen too old for somebody who eleven, so I'm getting scared, and I start backing away from him, and that's when he hollers at me to 'come here!' I walked back toward him, and he smiled at me.

"'My name Gravy,' he say. 'I want to see you again. Tomorrow, when you get out of school come up to 1103.' I said, 'Okay,' but I wasn't going up to no grown man's house. I tried to stay away from him. I knew that he sold drugs in front of my building, so I always went around the back after school. I was so scared of him, and how he was looking at me. A couple days later, he came and knocked on my door. I saw him through the peephole and jumped away from the door, holding my mouth. Mama was in her room, but she ran in the front when she heard knocking. 'Who is it?' she asked. I start talking fast, 'Mama, it's this man, he want me to go with him,' I try to tell her the whole story, but before I can really get it out, she swing the door open and say, 'Hey, Gravy,' all happy. I almost pee on myself when I see how mad he is. He put something in Mama's hand, and she run out of the kitchen, leaving me by myself.

"He say, 'Come on,' like he my daddy or something. I take a step back, and he scream it. Tears start falling down my face, and I holler for Mama, but she don't say 'Huh?' or 'What?' or come running for me. She don't come for me, Fe Fe." As she says my name, it comes out all weird, cracking in her throat.

"It's been like that since she started them drugs."

"What happened when you went to his house?" I asked her, terrified because I knew the answer already. She just looked at me for a moment, then she started crying again.

"Sometimes they make me stay with them for days."

I scooted closer to Tonya and hugged her, crying into her hair. I knew that her mama wasn't kind and responsible like mine, but things were worse for her than I could've ever imagined.

Stacia and Meka and probably a bunch of other people tried to make it look like Tonya was a hoe, but I knew even then that Tonya was just a kid, and what was happening to her was sexual abuse. I let her go and looked at her and said, "We gotta tell my mama." She slid across the floor away from me and started talking real fast. "You can't tell nobody. They say they gone kill my mama if anybody find out."

"My mama said that adults only ask kids to keep secrets when they doing something wrong. Tell me who said they'd kill your mama."

"No, Fe Fe!"

"But, Tonya, if we tell somebody, it'll stop."

"No, it won't," she said, and then she begged me not to tell. I told her that I wouldn't, but I knew that it was a lie.

"If you need to hide or something, you can stay with us."

She smiled big and said, "Okay."

On the way out of her dark, empty apartment, I saw the Barbie doll that I'd given her. It was naked and lying in the corner on the floor.

Back on the porch, it seemed like the sun shone brighter than I'd ever noticed. I looked into the playground at the boys down there, and then I got scared, wondering if what was happening to Tonya could ever happen to me.

How many dudes from our neighborhood had abused her? It could've been any of them. I looked past the boys and took a long look at Tonya's old building, still standing but broken in half. They had wrapped that yellow caution tape around it, trying to tell people that it was dangerous to play by the mess of bricks, and I thought about how silly that was. That was the most dangerous part of the block? The demolished building? There wasn't enough caution tape in the world for our neighborhood.

NINETEEN

The Wild

After Tonya told me her secret, I had more headaches. Some days, I didn't even realize I was worrying until wiggling lights started creeping across the room or I got that funny feeling in my throat that nausea created. Most days, I'd catch it before the pain in my head started. Mama always helped me lie down and put something over my eyes. I could tell she was still sad that Meechie had left, but now that I was having migraines, she didn't go in her room and shut the door like she did before. For the few weeks she was all short with me, answering questions quick, and not getting all in my business, I wondered if I'd ever see my sweet mama again. Then she did come back. Maybe she remembered that she still had a kid at home, and that I still needed her.

We went to a festival in Grant Park; we hadn't been back there since the day that she'd taken me and my friends for the Independence Day fireworks, so of course, I thought about my friends that entire time. It felt like a dream, the memory I had of all four of us standing shoulder to shoulder, looking up together at the colors in the sky. I wanted to do it again, but we were no longer a crew. I sat there with Mama instead, my shoulders slumped, looking around Grant Park at all these white families who seemed so happy.

Quan's words were running around my head, but I couldn't figure out why white people wanted to put us out of the projects. I don't know how long I had been eyeing this one family, but Mama caught me and through her teeth said, "Stop staring. What's the matter with you?"

"They the reason we all gotta move?"

"Who?"

"White people."

She frowned at me, but my face still looked the same, mad. "Baby, it's so much more complicated than that." I just looked at her.

"Well, ain't, I mean aren't white people moving into our neighborhood after we leave? That's what everybody's saying."

"So you're listening to *everybody*?"

"Can't listen to you," I said, under my breath.

She heard me and yanked her head back, then just looked at me. She knew I was right.

"You can't go around being mad at an entire group of people. They could be tourists, visiting from the suburbs or out of town."

I thought about her words as I watched the seagulls fly toward Navy Pier and boats sail out of sight.

Then Mama said, "That day that you asked if we were Lease Compliant, I couldn't tell you, because I didn't have the answer. I was worried that we wouldn't be, so I didn't want to talk about it." She paused a few seconds, then a wide smile spread across her face. "I received a letter last week that said we *will* be leaving public housing! I'm going to find us a nice neighborhood, baby."

I covered a huge, goofy grin with my hands.

Yes, we would move out of the projects away from everything

and everyone that I knew and live somewhere strange. But maybe we would go to a block where people didn't shoot at each other and trees sprouted up nice and green every spring. I tried to imagine a new life like that, but it didn't seem real.

I was so happy to hear that we wouldn't be trapped in relocation purgatory that awaited the families with kids who'd been in and out of jail. Something was bothering me, though.

"You think my daddy care that they tearing down all the projects?" I asked her without thinking. It just slipped out. I didn't know what kind of look I had on my face, but Mama reached over and hugged me.

While I was still smashed into her chest, she said, "Baby, I bet your daddy would've loved to be in your life, but he's not well."

"Mama," I said, and the tears just fell, "why some kids get to have their daddy and others don't?"

Mama was crying; I could feel her shaking. When she let me go, her eyes were black, makeup smudged above and below her lashes. I reached up and wiped them for her, and she wiped my face.

"Fee, some kids don't get parents who protect them."

I nodded, thinking about Tonya.

"I wasn't going to let that happen to you." She stopped for a second, then said, "Your daddy had a drug problem."

My mouth opened, and my eyes widened. I cried some more, because I just couldn't understand why people like Precious and my cousin TJ had fathers who stuck around, and I got one who was a hype.

Mama pulled me into her and wrapped her arms around me. I was fortunate to have a mother who'd do anything to protect her kids.

———

I watched the birds fly and the boats glide around and the people walk by, and after a while, that white family got up and walked away. I told Mama that sometimes I couldn't find Tonya. "Maybe her mother makes her stay on her floor some days."

I shook my head. "She always says she's not home."

"*Always?* You've been back up there?" she said, her eyebrows high with shock.

I nodded.

"Don't you go back to that woman's apartment. No telling what happens in there."

I knew deep down that I should say something about what Tonya was going through, but I couldn't muster the strength to do it, worrying that something *would* happen to Rochelle, like Tonya said.

We went home, and Mama, worn out from crying or thinking or sharing too much, fell asleep right away. Even though the streetlights had popped on hours ago, and even though everyone knew that life in the projects got crazier at night, I took Mama's keys and went out there, into The Wild, this place that had taken my brother and friends. I didn't really have a plan and tried to pretend like it was any other time when Stacia and I went down to the candy truck. We'd get a few glances, but no one really messed with us. This was different; it was dark, and I was alone, walking straight through the playground. I ran down the stairs and weaved through groups of talking people. Some of them stopped for a second when I walked by or their heads did a double take. That made me nervous.

By the time I made it to the playground, I couldn't pretend this wasn't a bad idea. The playground at night resembled a set from a horror film, especially with 4946 all chewed up, that tape making it look like a crime scene. You could still make out what was left of the sliding board, but the chains that were supposed to hold the swings got ripped out of the poles. They were probably being used to beat people.

Then I saw my brother a distance away. I wanted to run over to him and get a much-needed hug and some encouraging words, but that Meechie wasn't available anymore. He didn't even notice me; he was laughing and talking to some girl, enjoying himself at the summer camp for gangbangers. Where a dude could be a dude, no mothers nagging or sisters questioning the stupid things you do, just cops, always the police showing up. My brother had signed up for an ongoing game of cops and robbers. He'd been out there for a few weeks now, but it looked like he'd really settled into his new life in the streets. Every time I saw him outside like this, it seemed to add a new crack in my heart.

At that moment, the robbers were at peace, hanging with their friends and their girls. I walked straight ahead, but I was getting closer to what was left of 4946, and wasn't nothing normal about that, so I curved slightly to the left and headed down the fire lane.

When you walked down the lane from 4950, you'd go by the opening of 4947, a building that was still full like mine, but the third and final building slated for demolition on my block. Mama liked to tell the story of how Mayor Harold Washington, Chicago's first Black mayor, walked down the fire lane, with his army of politicians. She said the residents, who'd voted for Washington, felt proud that he'd come back, to shake hands and inspire them. Every time she shared this story, I'd enjoy watching her face warm up at the memory.

I passed by that building, and people looked at me like I was a sleepwalker.

Then I saw Stacia. I almost walked right by her because I didn't recognize her. She had her hair weaved into a long, straight wrap, touching her shoulder, and these tiny, stiff shorts hugging her butt.

Stacia, the skinniest and shortest of all the girls in a huddle, and her sisters, Pumpkin and Peach, and those same girls I didn't know from before—they looked at me, then turned back around. But Stacia took off running, and I wasn't quick enough this time. She ran up on me, and though I had a good lead on her, she extended her arm out and scratched the back of my neck before I could get away. I ran so fast and hard that when I looked up, I was almost at 47th—two whole blocks from home.

When I got to the space where 4848 used to be, the old highrise where Stacia grew up, I wasn't sure I was even in GD territory anymore. With her building demolished, the power could've shifted to another gang. There was only one building left on 48th Street, and there were so many people standing around it that it looked like a party. I knew if I turned around, I'd look scared, but I couldn't walk into a building I didn't know. I wondered if it was where the Black Disciples lived.

I cut across the playground, and when I passed one of their sliding boards, this dude said, "Shawty, come here." Instead of responding, I bolted toward State Street, where there were blinding lights and cars going by. I would be in so much trouble if Mama knew what I was doing.

The number 29 bus zipped by me. I felt safer in the light, on a street that looked familiar enough. Then a car slowed down and started driving on the side of me. The guy in the passenger seat leaned out the window and said, "Ain't you Meechie little sis?" I nodded.

He frowned. "Get yo' little ass in this car. What you doing out here?"

It's funny when I think about it now, that everyone knew that I had no business outside in the dark. Later, I'd think about how I felt abandoned by my brother, when in reality, his new community of gangsters was watching over me the whole time. I shook my head from side to side, because I wasn't getting in that car. I ran down State Street, and they drove behind me, trying not to scare me but watching to make sure I was okay.

When I got to my building, I scanned the area, trying to spot Stacia. I looked up at the porches and didn't expect to see Meechie on the second floor staring out the gate. I ran into the building and up the stairs. He was talking to somebody behind him, in an apartment. His voice was different, all soft and calm. When he said, "Nah, I noticed you. You be doing your thing," I knew he was talking to a girl. I got so jealous.

In that moment, I remembered when Meechie used to make me sandwiches and give me hugs. I remembered riding his handlebars up and down the porch. I was his girl. I had been his girl my whole life. Now he had somebody else. He went in that apartment and closed the door. I wondered if that's where he lived. I didn't get the chance to ask him.

I'd only been gone about thirty-five minutes, but it felt like a whole day. I put Mama's keys back, so scared that she'd wake up. She never found out about my trip to 47th Street. When she asked about the gash on my neck, I played dumb, told her that I must've scratched myself in my sleep. She didn't like it, but she didn't press.

I took a bath, got in the bed, and thought about Stacia and Meechie out there in the wild and how I might never get them back. My brain drifted over to Tonya, and how even if I went up to her apartment, she probably wasn't there. All in Together began that day for real, and all three of them were out of the rope.

TWENTY

Livestock

There was nothing fun about the final days of summer school. I was depressed about both Tonya and my brother, and nothing could cheer me up. I didn't want to jump double Dutch or play All or Run G Run. I'd walk to school with Precious, not saying much, and instead of playing with the other kids, I chose to sit on this pile of mulch that was stacked up as tall as a car and watched kids running around until it was time to line up.

When the stream of boys ran across the lot, I thought about my brother, tried to imagine him as a younger boy, playing this game. A time when he could just be a kid, running freely with no pistols weighing him down, no threat of the police roughing him up, just free and flowing and boyish. I didn't have the energy to run and jump, and my soul was heavy from losing him to the streets.

And Stacia wanted to fight.

When she appeared on the playground each morning, I sat up straight, like a threatened animal. She'd been chasing me since the night that I went out walking through the neighborhood and she had scratched me, though she'd planned to do much worse.

She couldn't catch me in the building, so she started hunting me at school. One morning, I mustered up the energy to play All in Together. When we got to the part where they sing the birthday months, a bunch of people had already jumped out of the rope, but me and two other kids were still in, I flipped around and saw Stacia running in my direction. I slid out of the rope and bolted toward the playground monitors. I had a small lead, but she was gaining on me. The boys chanted, "Run, G, run! Run, G, run!" but it wasn't funny; Stacia had become a gangster, running with the older girls, and I didn't know what she'd do to me. I worried that she now had a razor or that she'd fight dirty and hit me with something that could cause a terrible injury.

We were no longer those girls who had crashed the boys' game earlier in the summer. She had aged, and I suspected that she was no longer just a lonely kid who bullied people because she had been unloved. I was convinced that Stacia felt like she had to prove to the girls that she'd been hanging with that she was just as hard. So I ran for my life.

STACIA CHASED ME FOR A few days, then she just stopped coming to school, even though the summer session was nearly over. It was as if she'd decided she didn't need school anymore.

I didn't see my brother as much either. He was just out there, in the wild doing whatever he wanted. Sometimes, I'd catch a glimpse of him down in the playground or walk by him on my way to church with the Browns. He'd acknowledge me with a small nod, and I'd use my eyes to beg him to come home and be with us. Once summer school ended, I spent more time looking for him out the window and through the gate on the porch. This obsessive behavior went on for a few weeks, and then one very strange evening, things changed.

First, I noticed that the breeze wafted around the scent of death.

Some people think it was whatever still bubbled up in the grimiest parts of the Chicago River, the remains of scraps of slaughtered livestock from the Back of the Yards just west of Robert Taylor. I didn't really have any facts on the matter, but I can tell you this: it made me think, *This must be how bad a dead body smells.* I'd find out later on that there were dead bodies all around me that day, and it would make that eerie thought, *This must be how bad a dead body smells,* seem like some kind of spiritual awareness that I am not comfortable claiming. Not even now.

It happened sometimes on really hot days, this odor, traveling across the city like a bold tourist, leaving no neighborhood untouched. The other thing that made the day notable was the absence of its usual suspects. From the very start of the day, you couldn't find anyone outside. This is how the neighborhood would look as we approached fall, with my building hemorrhaging families, but that day, I knew that the building was full, that everyone had chosen a hiding place and crouched there.

I kept wondering if Meechie had holed up on the second floor with that girl, and I wondered where Stacia would lie low on a day like this. I assumed she'd just stay in 1502. But I wasn't supposed to care about Stacia anymore, who was trying to be grown and act like her mean sisters. I looked in the playground, empty. The bass and rhymes, missing. No kids speaking to one another on maximum volume, screaming down the porches. Something was definitely wrong. We had choir rehearsal at the church that Friday night, but I knew, even if the Browns didn't, that we shouldn't

leave the building, that if we were smart, we'd get to our shelter-
ing spaces like everyone else.

The Browns refused to acknowledge these kinds of signals,
though. They kept their heads in the clouds, focused on church
business. I would hear Ms. Patty reminding Precious to "be in
this world, but not *of* it" when she tried to tell her about something happening in the neighborhood. Ms. Patty had even said it
to all of us one day when she peeked out of her screen door and
caught us staring out the gate at the wrecking ball.

She'd taken 1 John 2:15–17 completely out of context. It
warned about loving the world and the things in it. We lived in
a drug- and gang-infested neighborhood, so I was hyperaware of
anything that seemed off. This sensitivity was viewed as interest
by the Browns, so they went above and beyond to appear as if
they didn't even *notice* the activity on our block.

That evening, I went to the Browns' apartment, and they
were just singing hymns and packing up Bibles. Precious, Ms.
Patty, and I planned to practice songs for the next day's church
service, and Mr. Brown had scheduled a meeting with the dea-
cons. I wanted to say something, but already I felt insecure about
my faith. I worried that it would seem as though I didn't trust
God the way that I ought to. I kept my mouth shut and let the
anxiety inflate in my chest. But we all smelled that foul scent,
thick in the air. It crawled through open windows and skipped up
and down the porch.

We headed out of the building toward the Browns' car. Everyone's faces scrunched up or pinched tight. The Browns tried to
set an example, so their expressions changed to neutral, smooth
like they didn't smell it anymore, but me and Precious frowned
and giggled as we walked toward their car. Before we could get

in, a Chevy with spinning rims screeched by, and flashes of light sparked from the car window, the shots so loud they disoriented us.

We bumped into one another, like winos, confused about which direction to run. Ms. Patty hollered, "Car!" and we all refocused, ran the few feet to the curb, then jumped in. Crouched low, we listened to more gunshots, this time coming from all around us: our building, the shopping center, on the other side of the street at DuSable.

The shots seemed closer, because the popping grew louder, then stopped.

Mr. Brown started praying. We all grabbed on to each other, hoping God would rescue us. I raised my head up and peeked out the window. The streets were empty again, and that car seemed to be parked in the middle of the road, but half a block away, right across from my school.

Roady, Meechie, and Nook came over and banged on the car window. My brother said, "Come on." The Browns didn't move right away. They looked at Meechie as if he'd had a gun pointed at their heads. It was my brother, and no one could stop me from pulling on that handle and jumping out. I turned back to them and said, "It's okay."

They eased up, looking out of the windows, and we all ran from the car. Just a block behind us, there were boys running down State Street, and from the look on Roady's face, they were not friends.

I crunched over the hard, dry dirt that was supposed to be grass but contained broken bottle shards, and just before I was at the swings, I heard *pop, pop, pop*, and a bullet, like an insect, buzzed by my left cheek. I didn't slow down or hit the ground; I just ran right into the building and up the stairs. My chest hurt, and tears made it hard to see. I didn't look back, but I knew that I was alone, that no one ran behind me. I wondered if one of the Browns got shot. Before I could get out of the stairway, and run down the porch, I heard more shots coming from both the playground and the front of the building. I worried that my brother was dead. If this scent of death was an omen, if I would lose him that day. I always think about how he yanked me out of that Camry before all the bullets started flying again, how he probably saved my life.

I ran and ran until I reached our apartment and attacked the door with both my fists and feet. I heard Mama's house shoes scraping the floor all fast. She assumed I was already at church and, when she opened the door, looked shocked to see me. "Mama, Meechie downstairs" was all that I could breathe out as we rushed to the hallway. We heard more shots and she froze—her reflex was to run outside, after her boy, so her body jerked in that direc-tion, but then she looked down at me, making the tough decision of choosing one kid over the other.

"Come on," she said, and pulled me toward the hallway, where we curled into a position that I knew too well. Instead of tucking into Mama in my protective stance, I sat up straight, my brain trying to make a decision about what I was about to do.

The thought came back again. *Did Meechie get shot? Did he die for me? Are the Browns dead too?* I popped up and ran out the door, down the porch, down the stairs, taking them three at a time, then swinging over the rest. I heard Mama behind me, in pursuit, calling my name, but I couldn't stop. I ran through the breezeway and out into the lot. I didn't expect to see the police everywhere. They'd cuffed so many boys, and I arrived just in time to see them slam Mr. Brown onto the ground, and one cop had a knee on his back and his collar gripped tight in his hand.

The tears blurred my vision and the anger blotted out any

rational thought. I snapped my head up and down the line of dudes looking for my brother. I didn't see Roady either. None of the faces looked familiar, and that's when I realized that those guys were from the Low End, and that they were the ones shooting at us.

Three paddy wagons rolled down State Street and turned into the lot, wailing and flashing red and blue. A cop jumped out and walked around back to unlock the doors.

"Inside!" another one yelled, and the boys rose up, formed a line, and one by one they climbed up into the wagon. Mr. Brown, who was double the age of the other guys and dressed up like someone with business matters to attend to, stood with his shoulders back and a calm demeanor and gave me a look as if to say, *I'm okay.* His white dress shirt was caked with filth from the ground, the collar lifted up on one side as if he had been fighting.

I ran toward him, screaming, "Let him go! He's a pastor!" but someone grabbed me from behind and pulled me away. It was Mama.

An officer pushed him into the truck with all those gang-bangers. I scanned the block for my brother and still didn't see him. The sirens were painfully loud as the ambulance arrived, and that's when I knew for sure that they were coming to get his body.

Mama walked me back into the building where we saw Ms. Patty and Precious huddled together, crying. I had to find my brother. I wiggled out of Mama's grip and ran through the breezeway. I heard Mama behind me, hollering, "Felicia! Get back here!" but nothing could stop me from searching for my brother.

On the other side, the police had a second group of boys cuffed at the curb by the high school. I scanned the group, and that's where I found him. I ran toward Meechie, screaming his name. The police looked over at me, and I saw that it was one of the cops who had been in our house earlier that summer.

He put his hand out to stop me. Meechie said, "Go home, Fee." All I could do was call his name.

Then the police officer said, "Listen to your brother."

I looked at him and asked, "We just pick him up from the same place?" He didn't answer me, just made the face of someone who had bad news to deliver. What he didn't tell me was that my brother wasn't headed to a holding cell in the neighborhood lockup, but rather, to the county jail to await a court date that would send him to prison for six years.

There was so much speculation about this raid. People accused the cops of trying to make their quota for the month since it was July 30. Other folks wondered who had been talking to the police about the Buchanans' operation. It was such a mystery, but I'll always remember this date as the day in which I lost my brother and my crew of friends fell apart forever.

I watched them walk him into the back of the truck with the rest of the chained gang. They moved at the pace of herded cows. Mama steered me back into the building with a tighter grip this time. On the way up the stairs, we saw another group of police. We slid to the side, and they walked by us with a Buchanan parade: Gail, Roady, Peach, and Pumpkin. It didn't occur to me that Sweat was missing; my heart only had space for Meechie in that moment. We had lost him again to the police, and it was clear that this time they *could* keep him.

TWENTY-ONE

Last Tag

That night, as if our bodies were broken, Mama and I slumped in both posture and spirit. She didn't have words of encouragement, just hugged me and told me to go to bed. It was a little too early for bed, but I knew not to argue with her. From inside my room, I heard her wailing. It was all that we could do, give in to the sadness and loss and cry until we exhausted ourselves and fell asleep.

Mama slept through the whole night. Maybe, as a mom, she had heavier guilt and stress about losing Meechie, and it dragged her down into a deep slumber. My eyes eased open in the middle of the night, and I went to look out the window in the living room. At three something in the morning, I didn't see anything outside. The shell of 4946 stood there, haunting the block, but there was no movement at all: not one car driving down State Street, no lone soul walking around. It was as if the police had locked up everyone, and Mama and I were the only two people left in the entire neighborhood. It would continue to feel that way in the coming weeks.

I didn't see Precious that next day. I knocked on her door that afternoon, but no one answered. I wondered what happened with Mr. Brown; was he out of jail? Did Ms. Patty and Precious stay at the police station all night? Why weren't they home? The police would have no reason to hold Mr. Brown because he didn't have a criminal record, I rationalized. I worried about him, though, and how Precious was doing. I knew she had to have been torn up about seeing her father abused like that by the police.

On the tenth floor, there was no answer from Tonya's apartment either. So, I took the steps up five more flights to the fifteenth floor, hoping Stacia would talk to me, that I could make things right. I felt sorry for her and couldn't imagine life with a mama in jail. As I approached her door, I noticed that it was off the hinges and lying flat on the ground, caution tape snaking around it like a guard, warning me to stay away.

At the door, I said, "Hello?" and my voice bounced all around, because I was in a vacant apartment. I looked at all the holes in the wall and the broken glass: the cocktail table reduced to thick shards on the floor, most of it covered in blood. Their bar counter was gone, and the couch had a different hue of red, like the little Buchanans had been playing in paint.

I thought about Sweat and prayed that he wasn't a part of the bloody scene. I didn't see him with the other Buchanans. Stacia was an option too. I knew that the blood belonged to one of the two. I walked out of there fast, thinking naive thoughts about how the Buchanans would come home later, and they'd clean up 1502, buy a new TV, microwave, and stereo. The blood wasn't even dry, and already, hypes had taken their electronics. I walked home in shock, thinking trivial thoughts about replacing household items so that 1502 would look normal again. What I couldn't fathom at the time was that after the events of that day, none of us would ever *be* normal again.

ONLY A FEW DAYS AFTER the raid, I watched a semitruck pull into the parking lot. The movers began carrying out big pieces, mummified in plastic. I'd witnessed this scene over and over that summer. But then, they pushed out a dolly carrying a white dresser that I recognized as a piece of furniture from Precious's bedroom. It was odd to see it outdoors like that, out in the open and not in that small, private space where we'd whispered about boys and played Uno.

When Mr. Brown emerged from the building, his shoulders back, walking like a proud, confident man on a mission, a huge box in his arms, I could feel tingling in my fingertips, and I ran from the window toward the front door. I screamed, "Mama! Precious moving out!"

I bolted down the porch to 304. Their screen door had been propped open, so I ran inside, shocked at the empty living room. It reminded me of that day that I looked around Tonya's apartment and saw there was more space than furniture. There wasn't even a table left in their place, though. I heard Ms. Patty's voice in the back of the apartment, so I followed the sound. As I approached, I noticed that the bathroom door was closed. In her bedroom, Ms. Patty stared out the window, looking at the moving truck. I startled her when I asked, "Where's Precious?"

She snapped her head around and gave me a sad smile. "She's in the bathroom."

I stood outside the door, waiting for her. When she opened it, she burst into tears, and I reached out and hugged her. My friend since forever was moving. They were putting their things in storage and going to live with family elsewhere until they could move into their new place in the lovely Hyde Park. Just like I thought, her mama couldn't care less about our friendship and planned to move her out without letting her say bye. I gave Precious the tightest, longest, wettest hug, and when we let go, I didn't know what to say. She spoke up and said, "I'm praying for your brother."

I put my head down, and more tears dropped all over my outfit as I thought about him locked away. Now she was leaving too. She grabbed me, and again we hugged. Talking through tears, to the back of her neck, I told her, "You gonna forget me."

She detangled our arms and said, "You my best friend. All in together, any kinda weather!"

I nodded. Then I said, "But people jump out the rope on that game and go separate ways."

"Then they play another game together," she said, cheesing, her face rosy now, reduced from the bright red. She'd somehow managed to control her emotions, and convince me that I was special, and that we would remain friends even though she was leaving.

Ms. Patty walked over and told us that it was time. I hit my friend and screamed, "Last tag!" and she chased me through her empty living room and down the porch. I ran to my apartment and she stopped in the square. At my door, I waved at her, and she did the same until her mother walked up and ushered her away.

TWENTY-TWO

The Vanishing

It was Sweat's blood all over 1502. There were murmurs around the block that the baby Buchanans were taken away from Gail, Stacia included, thrown in "the system." The way people talked about foster care made me sad for her; it was as if she went to jail too.

I hadn't seen Tonya since before the raid, since the day that I sat in her house and listened to her talk about what she had been going through. I went up to her house again and again. One time, her mama opened the door, and before I could ask, she said, "I ain't seen her!"

That's when I told her, "I know what's been happening to her."

That seemed to shock her, and for a second, her face went blank and she looked a little scared, but then she just slammed the door on me again.

It was hard to talk about, especially because Tonya made me promise to keep quiet, but I decided to tell Mama everything: about my trips up to Tonya's house, the boys that came for her, and her mama being on drugs. It was like watching a clown change faces for a group of kids, but I didn't laugh at all the expressions that Mama made.

She wanted to be mad at me for going upstairs to Tonya's house, but she didn't have time. She got on the phone, and I didn't know who she was calling, but then she put on her business voice, and said, "Yes, I'd like to file a complaint for child neglect and sexual abuse."

I wasn't sure what all that meant, but when Mama started giving Tonya's address and everything, I knew that she was reporting Rochelle, something that Tonya had told me not to do, but I knew I did the right thing.

We DIDN'T HAVE ANY PROOF, but Mama convinced me that they'd soon take Tonya away from Rochelle, and that I probably wouldn't get to see her for a while.

Mama kept telling me that Tonya was better off, even if I couldn't play with her. She said that Tonya needed to get some help and that I had saved her. I wanted to feel happy that she was saved, but I kept feeling sad because everyone had left me.

"Where will they take her?" I asked her one day out of the blue.

"To live in a safe place."

"But where? She'll still be in Chicago? Can we visit her?"

"I don't know, baby."

"Then how you know she'll be in a better place?" I snapped.

She was quiet, and then she said, "Because I've been praying about her since the first day I met her."

I raised my head up and looked at Mama. I believed her. Even though she had never said anything about praying for anyone.

I had lost all my friends: Stacia was in the system, where Tonya would join her, and that would be awful. Precious had moved, her apartment boarded up with a black, wooden slab.

I STARED OUT THE WINDOW, watching people move out of the other building on our block, 4947. I had to look through those child-safety bars, and it made me think about Meechie again.

I could see all the way downtown to the Sears Tower. Its bunny ears pointed straight up and listened to the city. Usually, when the White Sox hit a home run, you could hear the fireworks, but by the end of August, after everything in our lives had fallen apart and none of 4946 remained, I could actually *see* the colors popping up in the sky.

It was strange to have a view of these things: skyscrapers from downtown and fireworks from Comiskey Park; they didn't belong in my neighborhood. You were supposed to get on a bus and go see these attractions, but downtown seemed to be moving closer to us.

On the porch, I'd look at the beautiful skyline and the playground and people moving around, but not without that gate in my face; at Robert Taylor, we were always watching the world through those bars. Like we were in captivity and wouldn't ever be free.

BY THE START OF THE new school year, all remains of 4946 had vanished, including Tonya's mother. Rochelle wasn't the kind of tenant who got a Section 8 voucher; so she was probably squatting in another building. I hoped that Tonya—somehow—had a foster family and was living in a better situation.

The construction workers vanished too, heading north on

State Street to begin demolition on another high-rise while we vacated our building. As people moved out of 4950, I marveled at the long semitrucks that rolled up, some days two or three at a time. More windows were boarded up with black wooden slabs, replacing colorful, flowing curtains. Hypes and gangbangers and random strangers from God-knows-where snatched them down, lived and worked in those vacant apartments.

Entire floors went quiet, sometimes pitch-black. This is how my block turned into a ghost town. This is how 4950, full of laughing kids and music with too much bass, became a haunted house, the essence of the families who occupied those apartments still floating around the wide-open spaces of the playground and the porches. I could almost hear Stacia screaming, "First!" Precious, "Second!" and then Tonya mumbling, "Third," just happy to be in the game, not caring that she had the last spot. This is how I left Robert Taylor: in the state of a haunted mansion.

The new school year started, and I began the seventh grade. I had Ms. Pierce again, because she kept her classes for three years, sixth, seventh, then eighth grade, graduating students she'd molded for three consecutive years. She wouldn't give Stacia's seat away. Maybe it was because she missed her; maybe it was because there were no other students she needed to watch so closely.

It sat up there like a headstone next to her desk. Some days, I looked at it, fantasized that things were the same, that she'd just run to the bathroom. Other times, I rolled my eyes at the space that she once occupied, but no matter my feelings about her on a given day, her presence was always there in our class. I could see her clearly, hair trying to pull out of its ponytail holder by midmorning as she darted around the room passing out papers or collecting them.

Even the trio that we crushed on, Ricky, Derrick, and Jon Jon, had disappeared. Ricky was there, his family hadn't left the building yet, but both Derrick and little Jon Jon, barely eleven, had joined the gang, working as Lookouts on the block all day, hoping to rise in power with that police raid creating so many openings.

Ricky's face reflected my sadness; we both missed our friends and weren't really trying to replace them only to lose the new ones too.

I didn't know most of the kids in my class, because so many of them were new, coming from buildings all up and down State Street, but we had one major thing in common: we were all being cast out of our neighborhood. I knew that my family was Lease Compliant, but some of the other kids in my class would continue to be pushed farther north or south until all the Robert Taylor Homes were knocked down.

Ms. Pierce let us talk out our feelings about what was happening. Everyone had sad stories about missing their friends who'd moved away and how they lived in half-empty buildings, and how scary it could be just to walk down their own porch.

The lunchroom had a lower buzz because the school was underpopulated. Ms. Pierce felt sorry for us, so she gave us more of her speeches. She wanted us to be tough. To stay focused. To remember, "If you want to be in a position where the government can't uproot your life so easily, go get an education, and you'll have more control over your situation." Her lines of inspiration got a little rhyme-y sometimes, but most of us kids drank it like much needed water.

I MADE NEW FRIENDS AT school, but I knew I'd miss the old ones forever. I kept the rope that we played double Dutch with. It was absolutely gross, but I didn't care, and Mama didn't either. The knotted ends had fingerprints from where my friends had gripped it with candy-stained fingers. I could see small blue stains from snow cone juice and red-orange smudges from Flamin' Hot Cheeto powder.

I braided that filthy thing, hung it from my doorknob. My hip would sometimes brush against it, setting off a swinging motion that reminded me of time. Back and forth, back and forth, a pendulum.

Though our future looked promising, and I was excited about moving into a new place, I was still thinking about the past and hoping I'd wake up and discover it was just a nightmare. I prayed for this impossible thing. When it didn't happen, like a mad person, I'd walk around the house, and even school, whispering my friend's names: *Precious. Stacia. Tonya.* It was my attempt to keep their hearts beating.

TWENTY-THREE

Away

Only a few weeks into the school year, I started having a recurring nightmare. All those sad stories we were dumping into a pile because Ms. Pierce thought it would help us—this *processing*—caused my subconscious to drum up something terrible that took years to exorcise.

In the nightmare, I'm watching everyone all tangled up in a knot, one nasty ball of hurt. They're right in the middle of the playground. Some of their bodies aren't even whole, but I can still identify who the parts belong to, even with these fragments of arms and chests and faces. I see Precious from midback to the top of her head. She's in a church dress, turned away from me, but I know her apple-shaped head, and how she wore her hair as a five-year-old, with the part going down the middle and two ropy braids with ribbons around the bottom of each one.

Mama Pearl's thick, stubby fingers grip her beat-up leather bag like someone would try to snatch it, which is how she actually carries her purse. Police sirens *woop-woop* in the distance, not a full wail at first, just that two-note warning. They're the reason that the knot of people are trying to snatch away from each other. The more they yank and writhe, the tighter the knot gets, so they scream and cry and push their hips forward, but they continue to be a glob of body parts on the playground floor, which is all glittered up with glass from broken bottles.

The glass pieces cut the people who're lower on the knot; their blood is sticky, so some of the glass clings to them. The people who are high up in the air don't fare any better; some of them get shot by pistols, because the people at the top have guns in their bleeding hands; arms stretch out, pulling the triggers over and over.

Every time a gun goes off, Precious screams my name, and someone else lower on the knot repeats, "Come on, let me get it, you know I'm good for it," a crackhead's mantra. Their voices tangle up, and then, up in a stairwell from a higher floor, Woody and Earl begin harmonizing an old Commodores song, adding to the noise. They sing the same five words from the chorus of "Zoom":

I'd like to fly away.

It sounds nice and sweet, their vocals, until the words seem to melt and sour, and whatever has them distracted is messing with the crowd too. The glob begins to spin like a globe, and I see more body parts. Tonya's in there. She's holding a naked, headless Barbie doll. It's the one that I gave her, but it's got these purple marks all over its breasts. The knot rotates again and tightens its grip around thighs and necks, and people start to call my name, and it's all my names: Fe Fe and Fee and Fish. One of the voices is Meechie's, so I run closer to the knot, looking for him. I think, *I gotta get him out of this mess.* I see him there, and he's scared.

Then the sirens whip into full voice, and people snap: the voices screaming my name boom, and a migraine starts growing at the front of my head. The sirens get closer, and the volume of my headache rises too. The wailing and the pain in my head talk to one another until little lights—like soft thunder—twinkle in front of the knot. The police cars, as if they're in a funeral line, drive down State Street six-deep. That's when I hear the boom. It blows the knot wide-open, and all the bodies fall out of the knot in slow motion, and land shoulder to shoulder in a line stretching across the playground and State Street and through DuSable High School and past Wabash, Michigan, Indiana, Prairie, and Calumet Avenues. I am on a tour, moving down the line, looking at the bodies as if I'm in a streetcar with exposed sides.

The police are nowhere in sight by this part of the dream; their sirens are shut off, and Woody and Earl, who are dead now, and down in the lineup, aren't singing anymore. Everyone is dead. Lil Man, who wasn't a man at all, but a boy, and the other kids and the old ladies and the gangbangers and the mothers and the fathers—even the ones who wouldn't claim their kids, because somehow, I know their secrets.

Ms. Rose, who sold us candy; and Mr. Muhammad, who peddled spoiled groceries; and Ali, who fried up pizza puffs; and Ms. Pierce, the giver of dreams; they *all* lie there, dead. I see Stacia by King Drive; her face is smiling, eyes closed. I always wonder why she lies there smiling, if it meant that she got what she wanted out of her life.

The other Buchanans are lined up together, one long row of the same face in different shades. Sweat has on a white tee with blood splashed on it. I still think he looks sexy, even like this, so my body always warms up, even in this nightmare.

Derrick and Jon Jon have smoking guns in their dead hands. In the dream, they've both moved up from their positions as Lookouts and are full-blown gangsters. Right around this time I start floating backward, out of the streetcar. Something pulls me east, and I am flying, looking over my friends and their family and random people from the block. When I reach the lake, I see Mama Pearl at the very end of the line. She lies there like the first and the last of our neighborhood. Her bag is gaped open, and a pistol with a pearl handle shines in the sun. It blurs my vision, and everything blends into one peachy color. I always close my eyes at this point and feel the heat of the red orange. It's a warmth that eases the pain in my head, and I float, up, up, up, and Woody and Earl's song comes back, but this time I sing it with them.

TWENTY-FOUR

Sheeping

The nightmare followed me for a few years, then faded into random add-ons to other dreams, the bits becoming less scary over time. Long past the series of dreams, I'd remember seeing Mama Pearl by the lake and the feeling of that warm orange color that took the pain out of my head. Something about it made me feel less terrified before I even woke up. I had to go through the entire dream before I could feel the color at the end. I'd wake up trying to figure out why Mama wasn't there and why Mama Pearl played such a major role in the dream. Now I realize it's because of the pivotal role she played in my formative years.

As they knocked down 4946, Mama Pearl had become a kind of history teacher in addition to a friend, filling me in, finally, on everything I didn't know I needed to know about Bronzeville.

"Way back before they built the Dan Ryan, State Street looked a terrible mess, with horse stables and muddy roads. There was peoples everywhere hollering all up and down the street selling things. Back in 1944, when I got here from Jackson, men ran up and down these here streets screaming, 'Watermeluh!' or 'Ice!' hustling things that didn't kill you.

"Then, here come these chil'ren hollering, 'Loose squares!' and 'Bud!' They got loose squares, alright." It was hard for me to imagine this slum; it was a different time, back when you actually saw horses in the city and a paved street was brick, not smooth cement.

That fall, I started finding excuses to go see Mama Pearl, asking her to tell me more of her memories. I even got up the nerve to ask her if it's true that she kept a gun in her purse. Stacia once told me that everybody in the neighborhood knew that she was packing in that beat-up leather bag, even described the gun to me. According to the story, as gangs began to form, and Mama Pearl began to feel unsafe as a single working woman, she thought it necessary to buy a gun. It would take only one attempted attack for word to spread that Lucille Perkins carried a pistol with a pearl handle, and she'd shot a man in the leg. People left her alone and nicknamed her Mama Pearl.

That's how that gun ended up in my nightmare with all that detail. But when I asked about it, Mama Pearl just smirked and told me to go get her a cup of water.

Sometimes she would come down to our apartment on Fridays for dinner; other times she chose not to make the trip, so I'd take her a plate. Earlier that summer, when I still had my girls, I wouldn't stay long after these drop-offs; I'd just hand her the food, kiss her cheek real quick, then run back to the square. Later, when school started again and the holidays were on the way, I'd tell Mama that after walking the food down, I planned to sit with her awhile.

Mama Pearl would tell me about how she'd been living on State Street since she was eighteen. Our season of the crack epidemic and gang warring was a small part of her lifetime. Her retellings always began in 1944, the year that she arrived. Of course, I've heard some of these stories over and over again, but I never stop her; these tales are not actually for my entertainment. They're really for her.

"Wasn't that many places coloreds could live back then. They had a little bit of city carved out for us, and it seem like you'd get off the train and a strong wind would keep you out of the North Side, push you right down through Bronzeville. Then it stop." She laughed at this, amusing herself.

We'd sit around, and she'd let me talk about my friends too, and how I'd lost them. I knew I could still find Precious at New Hope, where Mama Pearl and I went to church too, but she was different. She had a whole new group of friends, and I could tell that she was being nice to me, but she didn't want to talk about the projects she used to live in or the wild and crazy friend we used to have. She really didn't want to think about Tonya, but I was always thinking and praying about Tonya.

One day that fall, Mama Pearl asked me, for the second time that year, what I wanted to do with my life. I had an idea, but I didn't have a sure answer. I looked at her, then raised and dropped my shoulders.

"Black kids ain't got the luxury of not knowing what they want to do," she said, and I felt stupid. She kept talking, because Mama Pearl was never in the business of making you feel good when she thought you needed a lesson.

"Let me tell you something about these here gangs."

I sat up straighter, because I never thought Mama Pearl knew anything about gang life.

"You think these GDs the first gang round here? First ones to come for these boys?"

The answer was yes, I did think that they were the first ones. If not, then the BDs.

"When me and your grandma get here, we settle in. We meets peoples. We goes out with some gentlemen callers sometimes. We meets other ladies at Curtis Candies who live down in them Mecca Flats, these apartments down on 34th and State and Dearborn. So big, sits on two streets. Fancy architect built the place as a hotel for whites visiting for that World's Fair back in 1893. Fair come and go, then they tries to rent this fancy place out to Chicago whites. Know what they say?"

I shake my head from side to side.

"They say, too close to coloreds. You can have it. So coloreds move in. And make it they own. Open businesses: cleaners, jazz clubs, pool halls. Make a whole community. Then, the Illinois Institute of Technology say, I want this land for a school building. You coloreds gots to go. So in 1952, they close it and tear 'em down."

I looked at her. My eyes grew wider, because I realized that Mama Pearl was telling me that years ago, the same thing happening to us, happened already; that a whole neighborhood of Black people had to get up and leave because people with wealth and power wanted the land they'd settled on.

"Peoples got upset. They marched and protested, but they still put 'em out."

"Where they move to?"

"Other parts of Bronzeville."

"They make new places to fit everybody?"

She just looked at me like I was a big fool. Head all tilted, lips pushed out. "Child, Bible say, no new thing under the sun. This here migrating, it's all we been doing: them ships from Africa, them trains from the South, then this here moving from neigh-

borhood to neighborhood. It's sheeping. Folks gathering up coloreds and sheeping them this way and that. They done sheeped
your brother into prison. Trying to sheep us on further into the
South Side. But I wants to tell you about these here gangs.

"After they put coloreds out of the Mecca Flats, they knock it
down. But before they built these projects all up and down State,
we scattered past Bronzeville, going more east. Me and your
grandma stayed here on State at 43rd Street, but next thing you
know, we hearing about this here gang starting up. And this in
the late fifties, getting real big in the sixties. Back then, seem like
you could join if you wanted, wasn't these beatings on boys who
ain't want nothing to do with it.

"Fee, you know what I think? The boys who done already
made a plan for they lives, they do better than the ones who get
invited into somebody else's. I ain't worried about you and no
gangs, but if you ain't thinking about what you want with this
life, you might just fall into somebody else's vision.

"When I moved into Robert Taylor in '64, seem like the
Rangers was already starting up. You'd see a few boys standing
around. They wasn't selling no drugs, but they was fighting a
lot. I watched some of my girlfriends' sons get all caught up with
them.

"They was so busy trying to work to put some food out, that
they forgot to ask they boys what they wanted to be, and how
they was gone get what they wanted. So Felicia Ann Stevens, let
us figure this out."

I think for a minute, then I say, "I wanna do something like
what Ms. Pierce do."

Mama Pearl nodded her head. We sat there in quiet for a
second. I liked what Ms. Pierce did for us in school. She knew
what we were going through, because Farren wasn't Ms. Pierce's

only teaching job. She'd taught between the bookends: early education, where kids were fresh and innocent, *and* in prisons,
a season where people arrived scarred and mostly hopeless.
She stopped to check on us before we started talking about
US history or math. She got on our nerves sometimes with her
speeches, but now I know that she did it to keep us out of jail.

I told Mama Pearl that I wanted a job that inspired young
people, then I sat up a little straighter. I asked her to tell me more
about the neighborhood.

She said, "Well, wasn't no number twenty-nine bus. Chile,
these electric trollies skeeted down the street! You could see
the cords way up there in the sky where they was connected.
Before the CTA it was the Chicago Surface Lines. What else?"
She rubbed her cheek, like that would help her remember. "Du-
Sable was here."

I gave her a shocked face.

"Been here since 1935. Got to Chicago before me."

I asked, "You think they gone get rid of it?"

"DuSable? Oughta have a landmark."

"What's that?"

"Some buildings can't get torn down if they got built by a
fancy architect or for a special reason. I think DuSable was the
first high school built just for coloreds. That make it special right
there."

I take it all in.

"You know, Nat King Cole learned music at DuSable?"

"The guy who made that Christmas song?" I asked.

Her whole body snapped in my direction. *"The Christmas
Song*? Chile, Nat King done more than just sang about chestnuts.
Captain Walt Dyett was over the music program at DuSable, and
Honey, Red Fox, Dinah Washington, all kinds of jazz folks done

studied at DuSable. We used to go see them *Hi-Jinks* musicals. Baby." She stops and puts a hand on one hip. I lean in closer.

"DuSable wasn't just some school where gangs went and shot up the place."

"Nat King Cole studied at DuSable?" I repeated.

"*The Christmas Song,*" she said again, looking like she had something nasty in her mouth.

"It's why most people know him," I said.

She lowered her head. "Most people don't know a damned thing." We both cracked up at this. Then it was quiet again.

"So how you plan on becoming somebody who works with kids?"

"I could ask Ms. Pierce?"

"Good. You need to tell people too, that that's where you going. Something about a girl with a plan lets people know you ain't got time for foolishness."

"You was a girl with a plan," I said.

She felt proud and smiled really wide. "Now I'm a old woman."

"You still got plans?" I asked her.

"I show do! I'm gone move out of this here building and go find me some peoples my age."

I didn't like the idea of living far away from Mama Pearl. I'd lost so many people already. But I saw her at church with other seniors, and they had such a good time. I knew it would be nice for her to have a community her own age to spend time with.

MAMA PEARL MOVED OUT A few weeks after the start of the seventh-grade school year, relocating to a high-rise for elderly residents in the South Loop. She liked it there. When me and Mama went to visit her, she'd introduce us to her new friends, and they loved me because I was her special friend. Most of them thought that she was my grandma, and I never corrected them. She was my partner in crime. That's why, when I told her one day that I missed Meechie, she said, "Well, let's go see him." My mouth fell open because I was so excited. Mama didn't want me to go to the jail to visit him, but here was Mama Pearl willing to take me anyway, knowing how Mama felt about it. We both knew this had to be a sneaky mission, and that it had to happen on a church day so that Mama wouldn't find out.

TWENTY-FIVE

Project Mentality

After Mama Pearl and I talked about visiting Meechie, I wondered if Mama had already gone. I snooped around her room for any paperwork about the jail, and instead of finding any documents, I stumbled upon something else: an opened envelope, postmarked August 14, 1999, that was addressed *to me*. It had arrived a little over a week before, and Mama apparently didn't want me to have it. For a time, she thought Meechie would be a bad influence on me and considered cutting off our communication.

I tucked it in the side of my pants and went into the bathroom. There, I took out the letter and read.

August 14, 1999

Dear Fee,

First thing I want to say to you is dont worry about me. I know this a bad situation but Im gone be okay. Just like back at the building, I got people watching my back and I keep a lookout for them too. This place a lot like the way we grew up with people stacked on top of each other and the law popping up telling you what to do.

Its hard to explain why I started banging, maybe one day I can find some words so it make sense to you. I cant even say if I got another chance I would do something different. Probably hard for you to understand because you a girl and girls don't get run down the way dudes do. I aint saying its easy for girls. Yall got it hard in other ways.

Like your friend Tonya. You was probably the only person in this world nice to her. You and Mama. Thats what make you special. You care about people no matter what everybody say about them. God gone bless you for that. I know soon yall gone move. I hope its somewhere better. You about to go to 7th grade. Probably be in high school before I get out. Promise me you aint gone hang out with girls like the Buchanans. That was cool when you was little but you getting bigger now and hanging with the wrong people can mess up your life. People like Stacia don't want the kinda stuff you want. You got BIG dreams. Them kinda girls aint spinning no globe and looking at the world. They aint gone get out the hood like you.

Even when they move, they still gone think like people who in the projects. You know how Ms. Pierce always talked about project mentality? You ain't gone have that kinda mind. Gone do good.

Uncle Tim be coming to see me. He said he sorry for how he acted the day I got jumped in. He was straight up about feeling scared that his son might do like me.

We cool now. He bring me stuff to read and put money on my books. I just started the Autobiography of Malcom X. And he gave me this quote by a dude name Dietrich Bonhoeffer. He was a pastor a long time ago, but his words still work for somebody in my situation. Its too long to write it out but Im trying to memorize it.

You gone come see me? I know Mama might not want you to. I understand why. She just want the best for you. Its what she want for me too. Look after her. She aint do nothing but love us and try to give us the best.

I love yall both.

Meechie

TWENTY-SIX

Letter to Meechie

August 23, 1999

Dear Meechie,

    I found your letter. Mama tucked it away, and I don't know if she ever planned to give it to me. I'm so glad to read your words. Are you okay? I think about you all the time.

    I got a bunch of your stuff in my room. I took your crossing guard belt and baseball caps and some of your T-shirts. I want to keep you around. I got my rope too, it's how I remember my friends. I don't know what happened to Stacia after her mama and brothers went to jail. And did you know her brother Sweat died the day of the raid?

    Tonya got taken away from her mama, then her mama moved out, so I can't go knock on her door and ask her where she at. I miss her so much. I still see Precious in church though. I'm happy to still have her friendship.

    I worry all the time about you being locked up. I miss you and wish we could watch TV together or go downtown to the lakefront. I pray for you all the time. Mama Pearl do too. She got the whole church praying for you.

What I really wanted to tell you was that you gotta keep your head up, that God made you, so you special. You important and beautifully built.

When you get out of jail, our old neighborhood gonna be knocked over and scraped up, but guess what? DuSable and Beethoven and that little church that used to be close to 5135, across from the Currency Exchange, they gone still be there. You know why? Mama Pearl told me that they Chicago Landmarks. I'm writing this letter mostly because I wanna tell you that YOU a landmark too.

I hope Mama will let me come and see you. One day, I'm gonna get the courage to let her know that I found your letter. Until then, I'll just keep sneaking and writing to you.

I love you so, so, so much!

Your sister, Fee

TWENTY-SEVEN

A Reunion

Every second Saturday in September was Youth Day, so Mama expected me to be in church from sunup to sundown, but in 1999, I only spent part of that day at New Hope. Mama Pearl drove us to see Meechie right after morning service. It had been about six weeks since I'd seen his face. On the way, I thought about the time that me and Mama picked him up from 51st Street, and I wished that was what we were doing. This prison was a few hours outside of Chicago, a facility five or six times the size of the 51st Street precinct.

We got there, and I was surprised to learn that we had to talk to him through a clear window with a few holes in it. I recognized this barrier; it was the same bulletproof glass they used in restaurants on our block. I couldn't tell if they thought we'd shoot him or he'd shoot us.

When he walked out, I recognized his waddle. He looked bigger than usual. I said something about it right away. "You been eating a lot?"

"Lifting. Working," he said. "Got some muscles now." He smirked a little.

"Hi, baby," Mama Pearl said. She put her hand on the glass.

He put his hand up there too, fake touched it. "How you doing, Mama Pearl?"

"These old bones trucking on, Chile."

He turned back to me. "You look pretty. You ain't have to dress up to see me." He said it, but I could tell that he liked it. We were in church clothes, but I didn't tell him that. I just let him think we'd gotten fancy for him.

"What you do in here?" I asked.

"Build things. Gotta pick up big pieces of wood, materials. I work out every day too. You go crazy if you don't."

I wanted to cry, thinking about my brother trying not to go crazy. But I remembered how sad he must already be in there and didn't want to be the cause of more sadness. Mama Pearl jumped in, and asked, "How you keeping yourself encouraged in here?"

He paused for a minute. Then he dropped his head. When he looked up, he had that little smile again. "Be reading a lot. Read the Bible. Read some other books. Quotes."

When he said the word *quotes*, I remembered the one that he mentioned in his letter.

"Say the one by that pastor that Uncle Tim told you about."

He paused for a second, collecting himself like someone who'd just stepped up to a podium, then started. *"The essence of optimism is that it takes no account of the present but it is a source of inspiration, of vitality and hope where others have resigned. It enables a man to hold his head high, to claim the future for himself and not to abandon it to his enemy."*

I cheesed at him, proud of my brother.

"I say it every morning to remind myself that I still got a future. Even on the days when it don't seem like I do." We looked at each other for a second, having a silent moment of affection.

Mama Pearl cut in and said, "That's real good, baby." She asked, "Who said them words?"

"Dietrich Bonhoeffer. Uncle Tim say Bonhoeffer wrote it when he was in jail." I was shocked about this, that someone in jail could still inspire other people. I'd find out later that many important things were written while people were locked up.

For now, I asked him, "You know anybody in here from the buildings?"

"Lot of people. Roady in here with me." Then Meechie asked, "How school?"

"Good. Ms. Pierce say I should apply to a college prep high school."

"You should. You smart."

"Mama don't know I'm here. I wish you could see her too."

"She come see me," he said. Right away, he wished he could take it back. He saw that I was so mad that she'd come to visit him and wouldn't let me.

"Fee, she think she doing what's best for you."

"Like she knew what was best for you?"

Mama Pearl reached over for her cane and started getting up. "Baby, we see you again in a few weeks, okay?" She had a sweet smile on her face, but I wanted to hit something.

Meechie said, "Fee?"

"What?"

"I know you supposed to be in church." I couldn't hold my frown. We both started laughing. "You should wear that to school on Monday," he said, getting up.

"Shut up!" I said, then I put my hand on the window like

Mama Pearl did. He lay his hand up against mine. It was about a fingernail bigger on every finger. "Love you, man."

"Love you too," I said, about to cry again.

"Bye, baby," Mama Pearl said.

As we're walking away, I heard somebody holler, "Fe Fe!" It was Stacia walking fast down to where we were. My whole body tensed. I wasn't sure if I needed to protect myself. She was with some big dude. When I looked closer at his features, I could see that he had a Buchanan face. It was like she'd forgotten that the last time she saw me in the playground she tried to beat me up. "Hey!" she said, with a nice, big smile. I couldn't pull one up to match hers, but I came up with a pleasant expression and gave her a dry "Hey."

"This my brother Ed. Me, Moon, Jet, and Ty stay with him now. In Indiana, girl!" Her hand clamped on her hip as she rolled her neck. She was a Stacia in a relaxed, fun-loving mood.

And she wasn't skin and bones anymore. She had the body she'd been waiting for since the day I met her. I thought it was just because we were growing up, but then, as we talked more, she placed a hand on her stomach a few times. One of the times, she saw me looking down at her hand rubbing her belly. She made a funny face, like I caught her doing something shameful, so she said, "I'm pregnant."

Mama Pearl couldn't help yelling out a "Lord, have mercy!" and Stacia's brother looked off to the side.

"I'm gonna have it," she told me, proud of her decision.

I didn't know what to say. She wasn't even thirteen. I nodded, then said, "Congratulations," because she was so happy about it.

She gave me an enthusiastic thank you. The truth was that I felt strange about the whole thing. I hadn't thought about having children; I hadn't even had my first childhood boyfriend. She cut into my thoughts and asked about Precious. I told her that she was good, and that I'd tell her that I saw her. Then Mama Pearl said we had to go, and just before we walked away, I blurted out, "Tonya got taken away from her mama."

Her face eased into a blank expression; it looked frozen, but then I saw something else in it: the look you give your mama when you about to tell a very important lie. One that your life depends on. She reached for her stomach again, and this time, her hand remained there.

"I gotta go," she said, then turned and walked away. I watched her, walking fast, leaving her brother behind. It was the pace of a guilty person. That's when I thought about how she and her sisters and their friends were all hunting Tonya around that time. She glanced back at me, and I wanted to follow her, ask her why she was acting so strange. But just like that, she was gone.

TWENTY-EIGHT

Relocating

We were one of the last families to leave 1950, and that meant walking around a high-rise that was half-empty. There were even fewer gangbangers around because there were less people to sell drugs to. Mama escorted me everywhere. Gone were the days of running to the corner store by myself, and I didn't have any friends left to hang with.

Mama visited apartments when I attended school and announced one day that she'd found us a place on 57th and Michigan Streets; far enough from the site of the projects, but close enough to walk to Farren. She didn't want me to have to change schools when I was so close to graduating and going to high school. We also loved Ms. Pierce and wanted her to be my teacher through eighth grade. The apartment had a space for a kitchen table and a long hallway, with a little place off the side of the living room called the sunroom that didn't seem to have any real purpose. Only two other people lived in the building, and you could be outside right away instead of waiting on an elevator. There were no random people on the stairway, just the residents coming and going, and no sounds of gunshots.

By the time we moved out of the projects, our block was completely different. The season of gunshots had ceased, and the temperature was cool enough that the few dudes in the playground had to wear jackets over their white tees.

On moving day, I didn't have any friends to say goodbye to, but it was nice to have Auntie Nora and Uncle Tim over to help pack us up. Just like the Browns, a huge moving truck arrived one day and took our things to the new place. I caught Mama scanning over the building and parking lot. I couldn't tell by her expression if she felt disgust or sadness, but I knew that she was taking a moment before our departure to remember her childhood and also the many traumatic events that she'd lived through, especially losing her son to first a gang, then the criminal justice system.

We didn't talk about Robert Taylor much after we'd moved, though it was impossible not to think about it. I saw more of Auntie Nora and her family around that time. She came over to help us get settled in, and sometimes, I spent weekends over at her house. It felt good seeing family again. TJ didn't like the things that I used to do with my girlfriends, so I started to get into video games and baseball. And I made some new friends on his block in Roseland, which was nice.

I also stopped being mad at Uncle Tim because he wrote and visited Meechie, encouraging him to keep his head up.

By spring of 2000, all three of the buildings on my childhood block were demolished, their residents scattered across the South Side into neighborhoods like Chatham, South Shore, and even Auntie Nora's neighborhood, which would soon be clumped into the area now referred to as the Wild Hundreds, dubbed one of the most dangerous parts of Chicago. She and her family would move to a quiet suburb called Lynwood, buying a home there.

Because humans are creatures of habit, Mama and I would still cross the city to shop at grocery stores that were familiar, even if it was truly inconvenient to do so. One day, we rode the State Street bus down to Jewel on Roosevelt Road to pick up groceries. While at the store, this girl walked by me, then swung back, and said, "Ain't you Meechie lil sister?"

"Yeah," I said, already knowing that she was someone from the buildings.

"I used to live in 4950. We was at DuSable together."

Truthfully, it felt good to be called Meechie's little sister, even though growing up, I used to hate it. I would tell people, "My name Fe Fe, not Meechie's lil sister," and throw them a bunch of attitude. Now it felt like a special title. I managed to give her a little smile while I tried to decide if I should tell her the whole story about him being in jail.

The girl looked like she had it rough. There was a toddler running up and down the aisle and a baby seated in the front of the cart. I asked her name, told her I'd let him know that I ran into her. Then I started doing the math: if she went to school with Meechie, she had to be about eighteen years old. Mama seemed to have the same calculations going and looked slightly concerned that this young girl had two babies to take care of.

I started thinking about landmark status again and was convinced that people had probably tried to tear her down for the decisions she made, but somehow, there she was, still standing. I watched her roll her baby away, collecting the other one by the hand before leaving the aisle.

I watched her until she was out of sight, then I started thinking about Stacia, who at thirteen was pregnant. I wondered if this would be her life. I wondered who Stacia would eventually become.

I MADE NEW FRIENDS AT school that year, and I started getting involved in school clubs like Student Association and after-school programs that taught me about computers. When it was time to choose a high school, I wanted to go to the same school as Precious, but her parents had been preparing to send her to a college prep school since the day that she was born. All my mama's energy had been focused on keeping her two kids safe, so I hadn't been prepared to go to Whitney Young like Precious. Though I did get into a great performing arts school on the other side of the city, where I learned to play the trumpet and joined the marching band.

Throughout high school, Precious and I would live very different lives during the week, but we'd be reunited for prayer meeting and church on most weekends. Band sometimes took me away from church because we had parades on Saturdays.

For years, this was our life, building two different friend groups that never crossed paths, but still talking on the phone and going to the mall sometimes.

I tried to bring up Robert Taylor to Precious, and talk about Tonya, but she had stuffed our childhood deep down somewhere and wouldn't access those memories for nothing. On the surface, you couldn't see that I was still haunted by the loss of my childhood friend, my imagination running crazy because I didn't have any real details about what happened to her. I wondered about Rochelle, if she ever got clean and was reunited with her daughter.

By the end of high school, we both decided to follow the Seventh-day Adventist educational path, which landed us at Oakwood in Huntsville, Alabama, which is a historically Black college and university, full of teachers like Ms. Pierce—tough educators who held you accountable for your academics *and* your behavior outside of class. I majored in religion, to get on the track to become a youth pastor.

Robert Taylor had prepped me for a life of living in close proximity to masses of people, but the list of how the Robert Taylor Homes was so drastically different from college life was too long to make. Most obvious was how the campus felt like one big park; it invited you to sit on the grass or perch on a bench. My childhood home warned you to keep moving, that it was unsafe to stand still for too long. I would spend my first year on campus comparing both institutions, sometimes overwhelmed with emotion that I made it out of the projects, and that my trauma was manageable. I knew that this was not everyone's story.

Sometimes, though, when school got stressful, I'd get a migraine. Though as I grew older, I began to have fewer of them, learning to deal with my stress so it wouldn't overwhelm me.

After graduation, Precious and I both took a leap geographically and theologically and moved out to Southern California together for graduate work. We started out at La Sierra University in Riverside, but Precious planned to be a nurse, so she went over to Loma Linda, a few miles away, to finish up.

While she didn't like to talk much about the negative parts of our childhood, by the time we moved to California, our bond was tighter than ever, and unlike when we were kids, when our parents arranged our friendship, as adults, we'd chosen to be friends, and we knew that we'd be together for life.

TWENTY-NINE

The Whole Story

Even though we'd escaped the projects and resided in the land of sun and ocean, I couldn't help reading articles about Chicago's grim tales of violence. Sometimes, I even recognized the names of those who'd been attacked. Reading these stories always reminded me of things I'd witnessed as a kid. It wasn't until I approached my thirties that I stopped thinking about Stacia, wondering why she'd had that weird reaction when I told her about Tonya. I hoped that she'd found a better way of life and prayed that she could eventually find love, but if I'm honest, I never wanted to see her again. I was still, even into adulthood, thinking about Tonya, though, wondering what happened to her.

On trips home to the South Side to visit family—Mama eventually moved near the Browns and their church in Hyde Park—I'd pop over to Englewood to chill at some Black-owned coffee shops and restaurants. I'd read that a Whole Foods Market had popped up by Kennedy-King College and, of course, that's typically code for gentrification.

Englewood had the same kind of reputation as the Robert

Taylor Homes; when you heard about it on the news, it was rarely about the local garden planted to combat the food desert or the service projects that brought people together, but there was an article about a Whole Foods that deliberately set up shop in Englewood in order to be a source of fresh food and employment for its residents. Curious about this new location on my last trip back to Chicago, I decided to stop in and grab some specialty items for Thanksgiving dinner. Like so many things in my life, this decision seemed destined.

I strolled by the aisle of skin-care products, reading labels and smelling the scents of essential oils. Midsniff, I saw her stacking jars on a shelf. It was a profile shot, but I had enough detail to make a decision about who I was looking at. It had been twenty years since our little reunion in Danville State Correctional Center, where our brothers were locked up together, the day that I found out that she was pregnant.

I could tell by her features that before me stood a grown-up Stacia Buchanan. I didn't know what to do. I realized that I had been holding my breath, so I let a burst of air hiss out of my mouth, then ran through all my options: Call her name and have an uncomfortable conversation. Walk by her all slow, pretending not to know her, letting her discover me. I decided to avoid the whole thing, just leave the store. While walking away, I heard a high-pitched voice call, "Fe Fe?!"

I turned around and performed some terrible acting. I scrunched up my face a little, squinted my eyes, tried to act like I didn't recognize her. She tilted her head forward, grinned, then said, "It's Stacia! You probably don't recognize me cause I put on all this weight."

She rubbed her body to show me the fat, I guess. "Shit, five kids will do that to you! How you been?"

I couldn't say anything. I just looked at her. I nodded and managed, "Good."

She started unraveling her apron and yelling down the aisle, "Jantay?" When Jantay didn't respond right away, she called her again, and I almost covered my ears because of the close-range volume. Jantay finally turned around, and Stacia told her, "I'm about to go on break." Then she smiled at me, and it was pretty, and I remembered this Stacia smile, the expression of a sweet girl, full of energy. "Let's go to the café," she said.

We walked to the front of the store, side by side. She talked, but I read the labels of cereal boxes and drifted back to our childhood again. I thought about Meechie and peanut butter Cap'n Crunch and Mama and her boring Raisin Bran and the Browns and Cheerios. It was safer to concentrate on the bright colors and the people who once loved those boxes. I walked in a daze, because I couldn't believe that after all these years, I'd run into Stacia.

When we sat down, she made a sound like a deflating balloon. "Long shift?"

It was safer than what I really wanted to know: Did she know anything about Tonya?

"Yes, girl. These damn people and they Thanksgiving shopping," she whispered. "You look good, girl. Can you believe we fucking thirty-two? Where'd the years go?"

I hunched my shoulders and appeared to agree. But I knew exactly where my years went, made it my business to plan them, and mostly enjoy them. We made small talk, then eventually I found my footing and inched toward something real. "How your brothers?"

This shifted her mood, so she stopped smiling and said, "We lost Quan that fall. Got shot by some dudes from the Low End." Hearing that phrase, *Low End*, gave me goose bumps. The feeling included a facial expression because Stacia matched mine. Then the jig was up; we couldn't pretend that we weren't both sitting on some heavy memories.

"What happened to you on the day of the raid?" I asked. She looked around the store, nervous. Then glanced out of the window into the parking lot. I followed her eyes, then asked, "You want to talk in my car?"

She nodded.

Behind the shelter of locked doors with the heat humming softly, Stacia filled me in. "We wasn't talking at the time, but I went down to the square hoping you and Precious was playing rope."

"We stopped going to the square by then because we were hiding from you and your sisters," I told her, probably with more bite in my voice than I intended.

She felt it, nodded fast with a face full of regret. She paused for a second, then continued. "Before I could go down the porch to look for you and Precious, my little brothers and sister popped around the corner, all out of breath, talking at the same time, shook. Moon and Jet got these panicked eyes and Ty got both arms wrapped around my thigh, crying into my leg. Moon and Jet talking over each other, but I heard one of them say, 'They took Gail.'

"'What?' I say, then Moon repeat it: 'Police got Gail.' Moon face serious when she tell me, 'Quan say come on.'

"'Where they take her from?' They all say, 'The house.' I run for the stairs, but turn back to tell them not to follow me. 'Where Quan at?'

"'In his car, by Farren,' they say. I tell them to go back to the car, that I'm coming. Then I take the stairs two at a time."

While Stacia told me her story, my mind wandered again,

to the day when I walked into her bloody apartment, missing furniture and electronics. I'm twelve again and she is too, her face twisting and lips smacking the way they used to when we were children. I know what she's going to find in that apartment.

"On the way up the stairs, I kept running our stash spots through my head: milk box in the kitchen pantry. Hall closet in flowered sheets. Wall behind Gail bed? Peach kept a shank in the mattress, but I knew she had it on her that time of day. I tried to hop up them twelve flights of stairs without stopping, but my chest started burning. And anyway, I knew it was too late."

She stopped and looked over at me and said, "I always thought that if we got raided, I could do my part to keep everybody safe and out of jail. Maybe then my family would treat me different."

We both stared out the car window for a second, lost in our own reflections. It was sad to think about living in a family with so many siblings and none of them spent any time with you, expressing affection. I thought about my one brother, and how before he left us for the streets, he was kind. I felt his love. Stacia's childhood was full of rejection and hurt. Thinking about it all in my car that day, I was grateful that she didn't end up like her siblings.

She cut into my daydream when she said, "Police was all over our living room and blood splashed on the back of the couch. Then I see him; Sweat laying on the floor, on top of the glass that used to be a table, and he dead. His arms all off to the side, a leg bent back behind him. His white tee soaked red like it ain't ever been no other color. Eyes looking at the ceiling. I want to go over there and put him back together, make him come back to life. I hear the police hollering shit like 'Get her out of here,' and 'Kid! There's a kid!' but I'm stuck to the floor and thinking in slow motion. I get my head to turn and everywhere I look, police all in our shit.

"They in the pantry, they at the hall, they coming back from our bedrooms with bags of drugs. One of them got a sawn-off shot gun. I know it's Gail's, and that if she alive, she ain't coming out of jail no time soon. I try to look back at my big brother over there laying in all that blood, but somebody pushing me out the door, out of my home, again, and that was the last time I was in 1502."

My eyes were moist with tears, but her entire face was wet. I reached across her and grabbed some fast-food napkins out of the glove box for her. She dabbed her eyes and blew her nose. I tried to stare straight ahead because I didn't want to embarrass her.

When she finished wiping and blowing, I tried to look over at her, say something comforting, but she started up again.

"When I got to the playground, it was ghost. Breezeway, ghost. Parking lot, ghost. Then I see Quan's Impala parked up there on 51st Street. Moon, Ty, and Jet all squeezed in the back, crying. Quan kept the front seat open for me, and as soon as I hopped in, I whisper in his ear and tell him that Sweat dead.

"He shot straight down State with the music blasting dusties. I look over there at him and see his eyes all shiny. He trying to be strong and not cry about our dead brother. I start up too, thinking about how we left him up there on the floor, alone.

"We jump on the E-way and go out to Indiana where my brother Ed stay. The little kids in the back still crying and shit. I open the window, let the wind beat the tears off my face. When I look back at them, they hugging each other. They always been like that, them three, sticking together, keeping each other company. I look out the open window and watch cars go by us. I know ain't none of them people got problems like us, they ain't running away from nothing like this."

Then just like that, she stopped talking. I wanted to know so many things, mostly if she'd heard something about Tonya. It seemed insensitive to ask. I knew that her mind was still on Sweat.

"They killed Quan right before the end of that year. We was gone set a place for him at Christmas dinner, but he ain't make it."

"I'm sorry," I offer. She cut her eyes over at me but didn't turn her head.

"I gotta get back to work, can you come back this time tomorrow?" I didn't want to, so I searched around for a lie, but then she said, "I want to give you something," and curiosity made me nod my head.

She opened the door, let in a blast of wind that seemed to clear out the ghosts of Robert Taylor's past, and I drove away, planning to ask her about Tonya when I came back.

I WENT TO THE CAFÉ the next day to meet her, sat up at the counter, and when the time came for her to show up, she appeared down the cereal aisle, walking toward me, but then she stopped and turned around, as if to go back. Finally, she reset and walked in my direction again.

She had a book in her hand. I thought, *Really? You want to make a novel recommendation?* As she got closer, I noticed that the book was thin. She threw it on the counter, then scurried away, disappearing into the thick crowd of Thanksgiving shoppers.

I picked it up and saw that it wasn't a novel. It was a journal. I thought back to that fateful day that we met Tonya, and Stacia ended up in my bedroom. I wondered if seeing my journal might have encouraged her to keep one for herself.

It was pretty beat up, like Bibles people spend a lot of time with. I flipped through it and saw that the first entries were from 1999. They covered the day of the raid through a little over the first year after we'd all left Robert Taylor. My eyes scanned the entry from July 30, and I saw some of the same details that she told me in the car, but then, a few pages later, there was a part about Tonya:

I kept going up the stairs and that's when I saw somebody small, crumpled in the corner. It was Tonya. Her face all bloody and body slumped to the side. I jump back and have to catch myself on the banister, cause I'm falling backward. I got confused, cause we beat her up and slashed her face bad, but somebody had shot her in the chest, and all this blood was on the walls and the ground.

I dropped the book like suddenly it'd grown too hot to hold. Tonya had been killed, not sent to foster care. A woman next to me picked it up and handed it to me. I flinched and grabbed it from her, wiping away tears as I stumbled out of the store.

On the drive back to Mama's apartment, where I'd have to break the news to her, my vision began to look weird, and squiggly lines appeared and danced, while the air began to curl in the back of my throat.

THIRTY

The Happiest Place

After Thanksgiving, I returned to my life in California, thinking that run-in with Stacia could be stuffed back down where I kept a ton of thoughts about Robert Taylor, but the experience in the store and that book I'd brought home with me had changed my life.

One night I burst into tears replaying the images that Stacia wrote about in her journal about how she and her sisters and new friends had jumped on Tonya, brutally beating her and cutting her face. Mama had called and reported Rochelle too late. I went through that entire journal, reading and rereading the part about Tonya's attack.

A rage for Stacia bubbled in me, even as I studied divinity and tried to get closer to God. I remembered how she stomped out that woman Tootie with a mob of people and didn't seem to feel the tiniest remorse about it; afterward, she never even acknowledged what she'd done.

I WASN'T ABLE TO SAVE Tonya that summer, but I swore I'd work really hard to save other kids who were being ignored and abused. I wasn't sure how I'd get there at first, but then I watched the Brown family use pastoral ministry to feed people in the neighborhood over the years. They visited sick and shut-in elders and offered resources to teens.

Stacia's journal made me change my major from social work to the Master of Divinity program. I wanted to help inner-city youth and get resources out to rape victims. I began working with churches that had outreach programs in underserved communities and started to lean into my trauma from childhood.

I started talking about Stacia to my therapist and praying for her during church services. I'd gone through her journal backward and forward and knew enough about the Buchanans to write all their biographies. I read it often. Cried into it. The parts about Tonya were the worst to read. And the entries where Stacia talks about what she did when she ran off into the wild with her sisters and mourns for her brothers, Sweat and Quan, or questions whether she could ever give love to a child, made me cry too. It's a book of tragedies, tales of that place that I convinced myself I'd forgotten. The words in that journal sprang up, like a pop-up book, each page a three-dimensional telling of events that a twelve-year-old shouldn't hear about, definitely shouldn't experience.

According to the journal, Stacia had never entered the system, but rather, moved into a loving home with her brother, his wife, and her younger siblings. Some days, I was happy for her. Other times, I felt like she should've suffered for her part in Tonya's attack. I've been challenged over the years by Stacia, my relationship with God a hindrance in my natural inclination to hate her with my entire being.

I held on to that book while I watched Stacia squirm. She didn't realize she'd given her journal to someone who lived over two thousand miles away. Maybe she figured she'd get it back whenever I returned to the store to confront her, but I planned to process what she'd given me, to think long and hard about what it meant.

AFTER IT'D BEEN SEVERAL MONTHS, she found me online, sent me friend requests, trying her best to get me to talk to her. But I enjoyed her misery. By the second year, it was just too hard to think about what happened in those buildings, so I tucked the journal in a box, put that in a closet, and threw some things on top of it. Time passed, and she stopped reaching out. Then something happened; I started to feel guilt. It pissed me off, but I knew that I had to talk to her, eventually give back her incriminating tales.

THIRTY-ONE

Ed's House

September 10, 1999

2:02 p.m.

Ed stay on this street of houses that make a U shape, not stacked up like projects.

They say I met him before, but I was a baby. The minute I look at him, I can tell right away he one of us. Quan look like a little boy standing in front of him. Ed, a foot taller, got muscles and tattoos and a head the size of a Rot. Next to him is some chick, and two girls who look my age, but that's about it. They dressed all dumb, everything covered, shorts too long. Look like they going to a church thing. They got some long hair. It ain't no good hair, but it's long, at they shoulders. I decide right away not to like them bitches.

Ed and Quan do that handshake that turn into a hug, but they don't let go like you supposed to. Quan crying. I don't know what to do. Ed look over at his girl.

"Take them somewhere." She grab Moon, Jet, and Ty, and her girls, and look at me. It's just a look, not bossy, or I woulda snapped. I just turn my head, and she know I ain't going no damned where. They all walk to this big truck

parked outside. Ed look me in the eye, and I tell him with no words that I ain't no little ass kid. We go in the house and sit down. Quan say, "Sweat dead. Police shot him."

As soon as the words come out, I see him again, his arms and legs spread all over the place, same way he sleep. Ed drop his head, start rubbing his waves over and over. When he look up, his face wet. I find out Sweat was Ed's favorite too, that Ed the reason Sweat loved books so much. We talk about Sweat later, after Quan go back to the block where he gone stay with some girl. Quan tell him that everybody else in jail. When he say it, that shit hit me hard. All my sisters, Roady, Gail, all locked up. Gone be for a while cause Quan say they all had weapon on them.

This my new life. All the Buchanans I see, the new Indiana Crew, they all I'm gonna get. I went to they school for a minute, which was lame as hell. I missed Farren, though, and Ms. Pierce. I get in a fight first week of school.

You know what Ed do? He sit me down, ask me how I'm doing. Why I feel like boxing. Ask me if it's cause of Sweat or cause I miss my other brothers and sisters? The buildings? My friends? I just look at his ass. We both know it's all of that shit. He start telling me about Sweat. How when Gail had him in her stomach, she let him feel the kicking. How the day he came out, he got to name him Michael, cause some talented people, even a angel, got that name. I want to throw Ed all kinds of attitude, but it's hard. He hurting too, and I like when he talk to me. He look me in the face, like Ms. Pierce. Come to find me after school so he can ask me what happened that day. I try to be nice to his daughters after a while cause I like Ed and wanna stay. Ain't nothing to go back to on State Street anyway. Just a bloody apartment where my brother died.

THIRTY-TWO

What Mamas Do

October 7, 1999

Doctor say I got a baby growing inside me. My choices follow me across the state to Indiana. I feel stupid. None of my sisters got babies cause Gail had them on birth control. "I'm the only one having babies in this bitch," Gail say. I get scared and shame, and when me and Tracy sit down and tell Ed, he brush his waves again, but then he look at me and ask, "What you want to do?" I almost fall out my chair, cause don't nobody ask me shit. I don't understand what he wanna know, cause when you get pregnant, you have a damned baby.

"You could have it and we all raise it. You could have it, and give it up for adoption. You could not have it." The last thing he say make me suck in a big breath. It surprise me that I care about somebody I just found out about. That's why giving it away ain't happening. I say, "I wanna have it." He nod, grab Tracy hand.

It's weird looking at a mama and daddy together; I only saw one couple in the projects, just Precious mama and daddy. Ed and Tracy do shit together and they talk to you separate too. I think it might be nice to have a mama and a daddy, even though it's really my brother and sister-in-law. I look down *at my stomach. It ain't big, but somebody in there. They ain't got no daddy. Just a mama. I could tell the baby daddy, but I don't know if I want to.*

You know who I wanna tell? Gail. For what, I don't know. But I'm about to have a baby, and I wanna tell my mama. Ed drive me all the way back to Illinois where she locked up. He say he ain't seen her in years, that when he left the projects, she got so pissed at him. He stacked up his paper, then dipped and she ain't never forgive him for that. He was good at being a thug, I guess. Gail had Ed when she was thirteen. He was around for a lot of gang shit she set up, was her first soldier. He try to warn me that she ain't gone be nice. That now that she locked up, she might be even meaner than before. She know she might have to serve over thirty years for all the guns and drugs they found in our house, and for masterminding the gang activity on our block. I nod and get scared.

When we get there, I think right away how ugly it is. How everything a dirty gray color or dingy white or metal. It's loud and echoey and I can't imagine Gail and my sisters living there. We sit at these tables and Gail come stomping over, a bear in cornrows. She sit down, look at Ed, say, "What?" She don't even look my way. Don't say, "Hey baby, I miss you. How you been?"

I speak up and ask her, "How you doing." She look at me, got a fake smile on. It's like she impressed that I can talk. "Fuck you think?" she say. We go back to our usual way, where she make me feel stupid, and I don't say much.

"Why y'all here? Come to put something on my books?" Ed frown up. "You still my damn mama," he say. She hunch her shoulders and say, "Nigga, if you say so." Ed just shake his head, but he ain't fazed by how mean she being. I came to tell

her I'm pregnant. To get some encouragement or some words to make me feel better. We just sit there, all dumb and shit, then I just spit it out, "I'm gonna have a baby." Her eyes get wide, like she proud of me. Then she say, "I guess you ain't as dumb as you look." I start crying and Ed stand up, put his hand on my back, and pushed me out of there. I look back at her and she laughing. That's when I choose. Cause I know Ms. Pierce wouldn't never say something so mean. I ask him if he can take me up to Farren to see her.

THIRTY-THREE

The Living & the Dead

October 22, 1999

Saw Ms. Pierce today. Me and Ed go up to Farren, and the school look the damn same. Even smell the same. The butter from them damn lunchroom cookies hit you in the face as soon as you in the school. We go to the main office. It's some of the same people in there. This lady I couldn't never stand say, "Buchanan?" like she can't be seeing right. I know she seen what happened to my family on the news.

She looking up at Ed, all scared. Guess she think he come to get me back in they stupid school. "Ms. Pierce here?" was all I said, cause I ain't got time for this. She jump on the phone, call up to the classroom. I'm so nervous. She hang up, say, "No answer." She got this nice-nasty smile. I roll my eyes, snatch away.

We about to leave, but I tell Ed, "I'll be back." He sit in the office, and I walk out, and up the stairs to where my old classroom at. On the second floor, some ladies standing on the other end of the long hallway, just talking. I'm walking up on them. Then, I hear Ms. Pierce voice holler, "My baby!" My eyes start stinging. She way down the hall, but she got that can of Pepsi in her hand. I know her walk. She always switching. Still ain't got no hair. She hug me, and say it again, at the top of my head, "My baby. I'm so happy to see you." I turn my face, look up at her, and ask, "For real?"

"I didn't forget you." I smooth out my weave. A new habit now that I got hair. She squeeze me tight. Then when she let go, here come that question, "You living?" I don't know what to do with it, so I ask, "What you mean?"

"I mean exactly what I asked. Are. You. Living?" I bite my lip and think on it for a second. She waiting. I think right away that I got somebody living inside me, but I know that ain't what she asking. Ms. Pierce sometimes asked us this question in school: Are you living? Sound real dumb at first, because you in her face, breathing, talking, living.

But then, she looking at you, and she want you to answer the damn question, like she for real want to know. That's when you get that she on something else. That she want you to reach down deep where most people can't get to and be real about how you need to get your shit together. Whatever holding you down, making you feel bad. She asked me that day, and right away, I got it. It make me think about how you can be alive, but dead. Then there's the dead that's really dead and gone, and if you ain't dead and gone, ain't no fucking reason you ought to be out here just alive.

Most of my family living big, but in jail. They got they own kingdom and shit, where they play and fight and rule, but they like monkeys in a zoo. They don't even see the bars until people visit and tap on them. That's when they remember there's people on the other side. Ms. Pierce come tapping on my bars with that damn question, and then, I don't feel so free either.

I know this baby coming, and I got a lot to think about before it get here. I don't tell her about the baby that day. I just let her love on me. I take her downstairs to meet my brother. She get his number so she can call me up sometimes, take me places. Before we go back to Indiana, I ask Ed if we can walk over to the building, so I can see it before it's gone. We cross the street, and I see it, 4950 empty and got that yellow tape around it. They gone knock it down any day, just like they did 4848 and 4946.

When some dudes see Ed, they get nervous, start yelling, "Ey Ikay!" cause they don't know his face from a distance. But then I hear Quan. He say real loud, "It's cool." I ain't seen my brother in months, since the day Sweat died. He come give me a hug. I'm surprised cause we ain't that kinda family. But this the new Buchanan way, since Gail ain't around. We stand there in the parking lot catching up and looking around, then I see it, Vulture City sprayed on the wall of the shopping center. It ain't a city no more, just half empty and half gone projects.

We leave. Quan don't want to come with us. He want to stay a gangster. "He get to choose," Ed say, when we back in the car. We go through the drive thru at the McDonald's before we jump on the E-way. I get a Happy Meal. Then that's it. Last time I'm over there.

THIRTY-FOUR

Haunted

December 20, 1999

I go see Ms. Pierce all the time now. Ed take me to her house in South Shore. First time I go over her house, I tell her I'm growing a baby. She asked me, "What you gone do with a baby?"

"My brother and his wife gone help. We gone love it."

"Bet Gail happy for you. Having babies a good hustle."

I looked down at my shoes. That's why she pretended to be proud when I told her. Ms. Pierce been more of a mama than Gail. We both know it. I got my period at school, and she the one who told me what to do. She paid for all my field trips. She the one been telling me I ain't got to be like Gail. She been knowing her since the first time Gail got locked up for running drugs for Ed daddy. Ms. Pierce was already a teacher then and tried to help Gail live too. But my mama only been interested in money her whole damn life.

Ms. Pierce say my next school gonna be a Alternative School, cause I'm pregnant, but it might be the best thing to happen to me, cause I'll get a little more encouragement and attention and be in class with just a few other kids who pregnant too.

*Ms. Pierce remind me, "You were raised by criminals,
your mama didn't parent, give you what you needed. This'll
be good for you." She make it sound nice. I get a little excited
about my new school. "They got teachers like you?" I ask her.*

*"Ain't nobody like me," she say, snapping that chicken head
around. We laugh. Then she say, "Yes, they bring in teachers
who ready to push you and get you back on track."*

*I'm still worried about something though: Tonya. I don't
know everything that happened to her, but we beat her up real
bad and I worry that I could still go to jail, me and this baby.*

*I still see her sometimes, all leaned over in that stairwell,
bloody.*

*We chased that girl for a whole week. When we caught
her, we dragged her down a few flights of stairs in the side
stairway. Meka learned how to box somewhere and was
straight up punching her like she Tyson. Then somebody said,
let Stace in there, and they pushed me on her, and I knew that
I had to show and prove. I could read the look on her face,
begging me not to hurt her. I dismissed that shit so fast and
punched her in the mouth. When I saw blood, I was proud. I
hit her again, next time in the stomach, and then I really got
into it, fucking her up like she was a punching bag.*

*Then my friend Valencia bumped me to the side with her
hip, real quick and sexy, and her hand slid through the air
like she painting, then I saw the red running down the side
of Tonya face, then across her forehead, covering her swollen
eyes. Peach clocked her one last time, and she fell down in the
corner. We ran up a few floors before opening the door, then
walked down the porch, trying to be regular.*

*Somebody went back and shot her. I bet it was Meka.
Everybody knew she had a pistol, and that girl was crazy.*

She went to jail the day of the raid too. Peach told me she got stabbed in there and died.

That day I ran into Fe Fe at the jail, I saw the way she looked at me, how she wanted to ask me about Tonya. Even though I ain't do nothing but hit her a few times, I couldn't talk about it yet.

I did want to beat her ass, but she ain't deserved to die or nothing. That shit still haunt me every day. I don't know why she bothered me so much. Maybe I was jealous of her. Maybe I thought I was better than her. All I know is that now I want to take that shit back.

If I could do it all over again, I would've stayed my ass on the three with Precious and Fe Fe, instead of trying to run with my sisters and they crazy ass friends.

THIRTY-FIVE

Snapshots

When I told Mama about Tonya, she reached for me, held me like I was a child again.

We mourned for Tonya's sweet spirit, and the fact that she never had a chance with no daddy and Rochelle as her mama.

Mama let me go and went to grab an old photo album. She flipped to a picture that I'd long forgotten about; it was a snapshot of me and my three friends from that day we went to the fireworks. "Let's remember her like this," she said.

Tonya's pretty face and rabbit teeth stared back at us, which made me cry even more. There we were, the four of us, on one of the happiest days of my childhood.

Mama freed the photo from its plastic sleeve and handed it to me. I'd take it home and frame it, and eventually, that image of my friend would take the place of the one that Stacia wrote about in her journal.

The next picture that Mama flipped to was one of me and my Meechie. We're really small. I'm maybe three or four years old, and he's about eight.

I'm holding a slice of cake in my right palm. Apparently, I will bring the hand up to my mouth and take bites. No one will stop me, tell me that it is unladylike. In the picture, my brother will call me adorable with his eyes.

I am grateful, to this day, that he, unlike many of Stacia's siblings, has his life. It's still a tough one, populated with ghosts that I can't see, and ones that he doesn't know how to exorcise, but he is still with us.

On holidays, like magnets, we are drawn to Mama's house, no matter the state of his misery or intoxication and no matter how hard I have to fight to leave my congregation in California. We give each other and our mama that promise, to return home, to look each other in the eye.

After the summer he went away, he formed lifelong allegiances that kept him safer in jail and employed in street life once he was released. The man who shows up on holidays resembles my brother, and sometimes can access the emotion and memory of who he once was, but mostly, he is the man he decided to become so that he could stay alive.

On Christmas one year, we notice that Mama had enlarged and framed a photo of us. I can only stare at these children, because they look like us, but it's so hard to connect to their innocence after all that we've been through.

I'm wearing a yellow sundress with spaghetti straps; Meechie's in a short set. I'm five, he's nine, and we're pressed back-to-back, arms folded across our chests, grinning the way kids do, before someone tells them that the look is too goofy, that expressing happiness so unfiltered makes them look weak. This picture documents the last few seasons that my brother and I are children. It takes us back to before we are injured; before the demolition of all the structures that held us in place.

We will meet people; they will transform us. We will see things that will age us. That summer when I am twelve and Meechie is sixteen, we will lose so many things, so many people. Among the loss will be the high-rises that our family called home for three generations, but the high-rises aren't the most important thing we'll lose; that summer, we will lose ourselves. This photo will remind me of who we are, at our core. It's just a piece of paper, worn, even cracked in some places, but it displays an image of a boy and girl who are fully alive and thriving and will love one another forever.

THIRTY-SIX

Invitations

For years, I wondered if both Stacia and Tonya had had different mothers maybe Tonya would still be alive. There were a lot of devastating stories in Stacia's journal, but after I read about how Ms. Pierce called Stacia *baby*, it made the monster that I'd created in my mind a wounded human being, and I could no longer add to her torture.

I eventually accepted her friend request, remembering that so many years ago, she'd accepted mine. Almost immediately, like she'd planned it, she had another request for me:

"Fe Fe, let's go back." I had no plans to ever go back there, but the words echoed: *Let's go back . . . Let's go back . . . Let's go back . . .*

PRECIOUS AND I SAT ON a beach and talked about Stacia. The Pacific Ocean always reminded us of the blue waters on the lakefront in Grant Park. I gave her the latest update, that Stacia and I were talking, and that she wanted us to come back and go over to the land where our building once stood. Precious was quiet, but as long as I'd known her, she couldn't hide any emotions; the blood in her face would tell you immediately what she was feeling. It was anger that appeared. She was still mad at Stacia and couldn't imagine being near her.

"You don't have to go," she said.

"We can't hate her forever. Let's put this behind us."

She stared out at the water, a brow raised in defiance.

"I'm going," I said. "Let's go pray together and put that time to rest."

Precious had a calm face when she told me, "I don't think I'm ready for that. But you should go."

I nodded, and we lay in the sun, quiet for a while. We were both back in Chicago, replaying bits of our childhood in the Robert Taylor Homes.

I knew that when Stacia asked me to return with her, that I ought to invite Meechie. Stacia had asked Ed if he wanted to come. So eventually we told the rest of our families. We didn't know who would show up, but we gave them the time, and asked them to meet us on the steps of DuSable. Mama Pearl at ninety-three years old decided not to make the trip, saying she'd "made her peace with thangs." Mama said she *might* come.

It's odd that DuSable High School, built in the 1930s, remains a solid, stone structure. It's in pristine condition, and still a high school. Only a select group of people know that it was once the site of many gang shootings and violent fights.

I SAT ON THE STEPS with Stacia, Ed, and Meechie and looked over at the empty land where we all once lived. "Let's go over there," Stacia said, already rising.

It was the middle of the day, in spring, but we didn't hear any birds. No trees rustling in the breeze. We stood in a wide-open field; nothing new had been erected since the final demolition of the three buildings that once blocked the sun, lording over us. It was eerie that it looked like the place down south where my grandmother was once a girl, in a country area in Mississippi she only referred to as Jenkins Quarters.

The land had returned to its humble beginnings, back before someone decided to overcrowd it with bricks and gates and too many people. Mama Pearl delivered this prophecy to me that summer before everything fell apart. She said, "State Street gone look like the country again." Then under her breath, with a faded voice, she said, "Probably be the healthiest this land been in a hundred years." I couldn't imagine what that would look like, with two schools just sitting there, and no kids to go in them, but we stood there, two decades later, and saw it with our own eyes.

We made a diamond without even trying, the way that me, Precious, Stacia, and Tonya used to stand while playing Rockin' Robin. "Let's bow our heads and ask God to forgive our sins, to give us the strength to forgive ourselves," I said.

I glanced up at Stacia, and she looked miserable, so I placed my hand on her back.

When we finished the prayer, I continued, "We all stand here, alive *and* living, despite all we've been through, because just like that school over there"—I point back at DuSable—"we were made special, intentional—"

Meechie cut in: "We Chicago Landmarks."

The Buchanans were new to this idea, but they liked it, nodded proudly.

My brother, who had read this exact phrase in a letter that I sent him back when he was seventeen, had held on to this inspiration all these years, believed it.

And now, a hopeful, dreaming man stood before me. "That's right," I said.

Ed pulled a forty ounce of malt liquor from a book bag and poured the whole thing into the ground. Then we thought about all the people we'd lost.

THAT DAY, I ACCEPTED THAT the Buchanans arrived at 4950 broken and destroyed, that while they were guilty of some terrible acts, they weren't the originators of our misfortune. In fact, they were victims of it, just like the rest of us.

After a silence that we all needed, I announced, "My mama cooked. Y'all should come over."

As we walked back toward our cars, I noticed more people had arrived, and Buchanans of different heights and complexions jumped out of SUVs and classic cars. You could still tell a Buchanan at first glance, I thought, acknowledging each one.

Before I hopped in my car and started the procession down State Street, I saw Stacia lingering by the open door of her truck, unsure if she ought to join. I called her name, held her gaze, told her, "Come on. You've got to eat."

She smiled and nodded, accepting my invitation, like she did so many years ago.

ACKNOWLEDGMENTS

My first words of gratitude are for God, from whom all blessings flow. You are indeed my Day One; it is your love and guidance that make any and all of this possible.

This book blossomed from a short story written many, many years ago. It was nurtured back then by professors/writers Megan Stielstra, Eric May, and Junot Díaz. A million thank yous to:

The writers who read the earliest pages of this manuscript: professors Nami Mun and Joe Meno and that incredible squad of writers in my program: Julia Fine, Jazz Wilson, Alba Machado, Jess Millman; and the three writers who continued to rock with me years and years after the program: Todd Summar, Clémence Houriez, and Brian Zimmerman.

The teachers who became mentors, then *great* friends: Audrey Niffenegger, who I simply cannot thank enough for all the things . . . and Don De Grazia, the thesis adviser turned lifelong coach.

The people and spaces that provided community, quiet, and peace: the Voices Writing Workshops, Ragdale Foundation, Corporation of Yaddo, John and Wendy Wilson, Laurie, Paul, and CV Peterson, and Soho House Chicago.

The folks who let me poke and prod their memory or sift through their shelves: Natalie Moore, who took my call, and Theo Williams, the cool kid from Farren who helped me relive our playground days. Much thanks to Judy Martin for her resources and the Chicago Public Library, Chicago Historical Society, Newberry Library, and the North Park University library for holding all the necessary gems in their collections.

The NYC Crew: My editor, Liz Stein, for asking all the right questions during the editorial process, letting me dream a bit, and listening to my desires for this work. Thanks to the entire *Last Summer on State Street* team at William Morrow/HarperCollins: I appreciate all that you've done to bring this book to the world! And to the fiercely talented, passionate, personable woman whom I get to call my agent, Meredith Kaffel Simonoff: you are one of a kind and more than I could ever wish for.

Drei and Cam for being there through it all: the drafts, the readings, the doubts, the tears, the fatigue. Your love, encouragement, and friendship were necessary ingredients in this journey.

Shune, my original partner in crime, for showing me what strength looks like and believing in me and my writing for as long as I can remember.

The women in my family who taught me all about love and affection: Mama, Grandma, Yvonne, Inez, and Lisa: so many, many, thanks!

ABOUT THE AUTHOR

Toya Wolfe was born and raised in the (now-demolished) Robert Taylor Homes on Chicago's South Side. She earned an MFA in Creative Writing from Columbia College Chicago with a Dwight W. Follett Merit Award. Her stories have appeared in *African Voices, Chicago Journal, Chicago Reader, Hair Trigger 27,* and *Warpland: A Journal of Black Literature and Ideas.* She is the recipient of the Zora Neale Hurston-Bessie Head Fiction Award, the Union League Civic & Arts Foundation Short Story Competition, and the Betty Shiflett/John Schultz Short Story Award. *Last Summer on State Street* is her debut novel.